Katy stepped into Dad's path and folded her arms over her chest to keep from shivering. "Mrs. Graber has been with Gramma and Grampa for a whole month now. Isn't she about ready to go home?"

Dad's scowl deepened. He tugged the brim of his ball cap lower on his forehead. "Her schedule isn't your concern, Katy. Your grandparents have told her she can stay for as long as she wants to." He put his fist on his hip. "And to be perfectly honest, I'm tired of you making her feel unwelcome."

Katy gawked at her dad. "I haven't done anything to her!" Dad's eyebrows rose. So did Katy's irritation. "Well, I haven't."

"No, but you sure haven't done anything to make her feel like she's part of our community."

She isn't part of our community. She just showed up, uninvited. Katy knew her thoughts weren't quite true. Gramma Ruthie had invited Mrs. Graber to come to Schellberg. And Katy knew why. She just didn't like the reason why.

Other books in the Katy Lambright Series:

katy's
debate

KIM VOGEL SAWYER

KATY LAMBRIGHT SERIES

ZONDERVAN

Katy's Debate
Copyright © 2010 by Kim Vogel Sawyer

This title is also available as a Zondervan ebook.
Visit www.zondervan.com/ebooks.

Requests for information should be addressed to:
Zondervan, 3900 *Sparks Dr. SE, Grand Rapids, Michigan* 49546

This edition: ISBN 978-0-310-74755-0

Library of Congress Cataloging-in-Publication Data

Sawyer, Kim Vogel.
      Katy's debate / Kim Vogel Sawyer.
          p. cm. — (The Katy Lambright series ; [bk. 2])
      Summary: Katy, a Mennonite teenager attending secular high school, joins the debate
team, and tries to keep her father from remarrying so that she does not have to adjust to
having a stepmother.
      ISBN 978-0-310-71923-6 (softcover)
      [1. Mennonites — Juvenile fiction. 2. Mennonites — Fiction. 3. Christian life — Fiction.
4. Debates and debating — Fiction. 5. High schools — Fiction. 6. Schools — Fiction. 7.
Interpersonal relations — Fiction. 8. Stepmothers — Fiction. 9. Kansas — Fiction.] I. Title.
PZ7.S26832Kag 2010
      [Fic] — dc22   2010004345

Published in association with Hartline Literary Agency, Pittsburg, Pennsylvania 15235.

Cover photography: *Mike Heath/Magnus Creative*
Interior design: *Carlos Eluterio Estrada*

Printed in the United States of America

15 16 17 18 19 20 21 22 23 /DCI/ 20 19 18 17 16 15 14 13 12 11 10 9 8 7 6 5 4 3 2 1

Dedicated to Mr. Ed Gorsky,
my freshman English teacher and first debate coach.
Thank you for being such a positive influence in my life.

To every thing there is a season,
and a time to every purpose under the heaven
... A time to keep silence, and a time to speak.
Ecclesiastes 3:1, 7b

Chapter One

Katy Lambright scribbled frantically on the long, lined flow sheet. A ribbon from her mesh headcovering tickled her cheek, and she impatiently tossed it over her shoulder. At the front of the English classroom, Bryce Porter, one of Katy's friends from the Bible study group at school, cross-examined a boy named Paul.

Cross-examined. In the past two weeks, Katy had learned several terms related to debating. The words rolled through her head—*resolution, topicality, solvency, inherency, fiat ...* She liked the meaning of cross-examining the best: *Clarifying facts in a persistent, sometimes aggressive manner.* With only two minutes allotted, the rapid-fire ask-and-respond of the cross-examination period always got Katy's pulse pounding. Or maybe it was the fact that Bryce stood right in her line of vision that made her pulse speed up ...

No distractions. She couldn't miss one second of the cross-examination. If only she'd signed up for debate at the beginning of the year! Because she'd joined the debate team mid-season, she hadn't yet been allowed to participate in any meets. She itched for the opportunity to stand at the podium with the other first-year debaters and argue her case, just like a lawyer in a courtroom. *I could do it.*

The debate coach, Mr. Gorsky, kept time by flashing a set of white numbered cards. Katy knew timekeeping well. Mr. Gorsky had put her to work keeping time for practice debates until she became familiar with the structure. Now she was learning to keep a detailed flow sheet. Today that meant recording the plan of action given by the affirmative team for lowering the return rate of juvenile offenders to the prison system and the status quo team's reasons to reject the plan.

A petite blonde-haired girl named Vicki stepped behind the podium and spread several books across the wooden top. As the defender of the status quo — the present system — Vicki began to point out all of the flaws in the affirmative team's plan. From the determined look on the girl's face, Katy knew Vicki took her position seriously. Bryce and Vicki, the status quo team, sat on the left side of the aisle, and Paul and Marlys, the affirmative team, sat on the right. Even though Paul, Bryce, Vicki, and Marlys were novice debaters, they were already strong presenters.

Katy snatched up her blue pencil to record Vicki's responses to Paul's plan. Mr. Gorsky had taught her to use different colored pencils to keep track of the various issues and reactions. As the debate continued, her fingers flew. The flow sheet became cluttered with comments and circles and arrows. She abandoned her usually precise handwriting in order to capture the important facts.

The debate ended with Paul's impassioned plea for the judge — in this case, Katy — to side with the affirmative team and adopt their policy to ensure fewer juvenile lawbreakers would repeat their crimes and return to a detention facility. Then the two teams met in the middle of the classroom and shook hands, formally nodding their heads at each other before dissolving into laughter. Katy dropped her pencil and clapped.

Mr. Gorsky tamped the time cards together and waved his hand. "All right, gang, come on over here. Sit down, and let's talk." The coach always critiqued the debaters as soon as they finished a practice round. Listening to his evaluation of the teams' performances had increased Katy's confidence that she could be a worthy debater if only she were given the chance. But she'd probably have to wait until next year, if Dad let her continue in high school. Only three weeks remained until Christmas break, then forensics would replace debate after school second semester.

Katy flashed a smile and a thumbs-up sign at Bryce before turning her attention to Mr. Gorsky. To her surprise, the teacher was looking at her.

"All right, Kathleen. Let's hear it — who won today's round?"

Katy blinked twice and pointed to her chest. "Me?"

Her teacher smiled, his mustache twitching. "Yes, you. You're the judge today. I'm only the timekeeper. Who won and why?"

Katy smoothed her skirt over her knees as she gathered her thoughts. Seconds ticked by. Paul propped his chin in his hand, his expression smug. Marlys examined her nail polish, and Vicki glanced at the clock on the wall. Katy's gaze flicked to Bryce. He offered an encouraging smile, and she felt her ears grow hot. Bryce's nose and cheeks wore a dusting of freckles, just like Caleb Penner from her

Mennonite community of Schellberg. But Bryce didn't irritate her the way Caleb did.

She shuffled the pages of her flow chart and swallowed.
"I give the round to the status quo."

Paul groaned and slapped his forehead. "What? You're
kidding, right?"

Marlys sent a knowing look to Bryce, then to Katy. A
smirk climbed her cheek, and she sat back and folded her
arms over her chest. "Oh, she's not kidding . . ."

Paul leaned forward and propped his elbows on his
knees. "C'mon, Kathleen, you know that Marlys and I pre-
sented the perfect plan. How could you give the round to
Bryce and Vicki?"

"Because she has a thing for — " Marlys started.

Mr. Gorsky cut in. "Go ahead, Kathleen. Tell Paul why
his team lost."

Katy couldn't quite determine from her teacher's tone
whether he agreed with her assessment, but she was ready
to defend it. She held up her flow sheets. "See how many
red circles I have on here? Those are unanswered questions about *how* your plan would decrease the current
percentage of recidivism." She liked the fancy word that
referred to people going back to old behaviors. She had
no idea where she would use it outside of debate, but she
still liked it. "The arrows are for the questions that *were*
answered."

Tapping the pages with her finger, she continued. "Six
different issues were raised about the current programs
and their success rates, and these arrows mean they
weren't countered by the affirmative team." She dropped
the sheets and raised one shoulder in a shrug. "You failed

to prove that your plan would result in fewer repeat offenders. So I had to go with the status quo."

Paul glared at Marlys, who shrugged and made a *so sorry* face. He shook his head at the ceiling and threw his arms wide. "Great. So what about speaker rank? Did I at least get top speaker rank?"

Katy hid a smile. The four speakers were ranked one through four, with one being the best position. A team could not win unless their speaker points, which were based on their ranks, were less than or equal to the points earned by the opposing team. She knew Paul hoped the ranks had been split down the middle. Even in the short amount of time since she'd joined the team, Katy had figured out that Paul was extremely competitive and coveted the top speaker position in every round.

"I ranked you one."

"Yes!" Paul grabbed a handful of air and pumped his arm. Then he leaned back in his chair with a satisfied grin.

Katy continued, "Then I ranked Vicki two, Bryce three" — she shot Bryce an apologetic look — "and — "

Marlys made a sour face. "I already know. *I* got the four."

The heat increased in Katy's ears. Marlys didn't like Katy — Marlys had made that clear by keeping her distance and using a snide tone whenever she talked to Katy. Ranking Marlys in fourth position wouldn't win her as a friend, but Katy had to be honest. Mr. Gorsky expected it.

She explained in a quiet voice, "Somebody had to get the four. And you dropped your notes. You quit talking while you gathered them up again and lost several seconds of presentation time. That's why I gave you the four."

Marlys swung her long, straight-as-a-board dark brown hair over her shoulder with a flip of her chin. "No biggie. It's just practice."

Mr. Gorsky cleared his throat. "But practice should be treated like a judged round. That's why we practice—to make sure we're prepared. If you drop your notes, Marlys, you need to be familiar enough with your material to continue."

Marlys scowled at her bright blue painted fingernails and didn't answer.

Mr. Gorsky clapped his hands together. "All right, then. Good practice today, gang. And good assessment, Kathleen. You've picked up on the fine points of debate quickly."

Katy ducked her head, pleased yet embarrassed by her teacher's praise. The ribbons from her headcovering tickled her cheeks, and she twirled one around her finger. "Thank you."

Opening a folder, Mr. Gorsky distributed printed sheets of paper to the four debaters. "Remember we'll be going to the Southwest Kansas Novice Tournament in Dodge City this coming weekend. Both teams need to have their affirmative plans ready to go since you'll be switching back and forth between affirmative and status quo positions. Bring your travel gear to school Friday for the overnight stay. We'll leave here at eleven o'clock. The school will pick up the tab for the meals while we're on the road, but if you want snacks in the hotel, you'll need extra spending money for that. And, Paul, remember your tie this time."

Paul grinned. "I got a good one, Mr. G."

Mr. Gorsky raised one eyebrow. "Does it have Daffy Duck on it?"

Paul burst out laughing. "No. But it does have the Tasmanian Devil."

Katy wrinkled her forehead. "What's that?"

Bryce explained, "It's a cartoon character—from Looney Tunes."

Katy shook her head, confused.

Marlys rolled her eyes. "She doesn't *do* cartoons, Bryce. She has no idea what you're talking about."

In that moment, Katy would have given anything to have seen the Looney Tunes cartoon so she wouldn't feel so foolish in front of Bryce.

Mr. Gorsky said firmly, "No Looney Tunes, Paul. Stripes, plaid, even polka dots, but no Looney Tunes. You need to look professional, all right?"

Paul laughed again, but he nodded.

Vicki held up the paper. "Mr. G? I can't go to this one."

Mr. Gorsky frowned. "This has been on the calendar, Vicki."

She grimaced. "I know, but I just realized it's a two-day meet instead of a Saturday-only one. I have an art show Friday night, and I have to be there to show my sculpture. It's part of my grade."

Mr. Gorsky stood in silence for a moment, his forehead furrowed. "Well, we'll have to find a substitute for you then. Let me check the novice list." He strode to his desk, pulled a notebook from the top drawer, and flipped it open. Running his finger down the page, he began calling out names.

"Cherie Hamby."

Vicki sighed. "She'll be out of town, remember? Something to do with her grandparents' anniversary ..."

"Beverly Hilton."

13

"Had her wisdom teeth removed this morning," Paul said. "Ron Sattler."

Paul snorted. "No way. He's on academic probation— flunking biology. So no activities 'til he gets his grade up to a C."

Mr. Gorsky pursed his lips for a moment then said, "Teresa Price?"

"She's in the art show too," Vicki said. She began to chew her lower lip.

Mr. Gorsky shook his head. "Well, then, that's every-body."

Bryce said, "Except ..." Everyone looked at him. "What about Katy?"

Excitement fluttered through Katy's stomach. "But I haven't even done a practice round yet."

Mr. Gorsky slapped the book closed and sat on the edge of his desk. He smoothed his mustache with his thumb and forefinger. "No, but you've caught on to things quickly. What do you think? Could you fill in for Vicki this weekend?"

Katy's heart thumped beneath the modest, caped bodice of her pink flowered dress. *I want to do it! I want to prove I can debate as well as the other first-time debaters!* She swallowed and tried to speak calmly. "I'd want to practice before I tried competing ..."

"Of course," Mr. Gorsky said. "This is only Tuesday. We will have time for at least two more practice rounds before we leave Friday. But you'll need a permission form filled out by your folks."

Your folks ... Mr. Gorsky's innocent comment stabbed Katy's heart. She didn't have folks. She had Dad.

Her teacher pulled a sheet from a stack of trays on the

corner of his desk and held it out to Katy. She scurried forward and took it. Her hands trembled slightly as she pressed it to her dress. "I'll give this to my dad right after school."

"Good." Mr. Gorsky pushed off from the desk. "You'll be Bryce's partner."

Katy glanced at Bryce. He gave her his familiar lopsided grin. She jerked her gaze to the permission slip.

Mr. Gorsky said, "Be sure to let me know tomorrow if it won't work. We might need to pull out of the meet if we don't have enough debaters." He frowned. "This is the last novice-only tournament of the year—I'd hate to cancel."

"I'm sure Dad will let me go. I'll let you know for sure in class tomorrow."

Her teacher smiled. "Good. Now you kids better scoot out of here." Mr. Gorsky escorted the debaters to the class-room door. "Especially you, Kathleen. The bus won't wait around if you're late."

Katy trailed the others down the hallway toward the lockers. They walked in a group, talking and laughing to-gether, but she didn't join them. Her thoughts raced ahead to the weekend. She'd only been to Saturday events, and only as an observer. But now she'd get to compete—and on an overnight trip! She nearly giggled in anticipation as she slipped her wool coat over her dress and pulled her backpack from her locker.

Marlys's shrill laugh rang in response to Paul's teas-ing, and suddenly Katy's enthusiasm wavered. Would she have to share a room with Marlys? Her feet seemed to drag as she followed the others down the hallway. She wished Shelby or Cora or one of her other friends were on the debate team. But they all said speaking in front of people made them too nervous. Speaking in front of people didn't bother Katy. The teacher she'd had in Schellberg made students recite in front of the class all the time, so she was used to it. But the thought of being stuck in a hotel room alone with Marlys made her stomach churn.

When they reached the front doors of the school, Bryce sent a smile over his shoulder. "'Bye, Katy. See you tomorrow morning at Bible study, right?"

Katy nodded. She enjoyed meeting with the Christian students at Salina High North for a time of Bible study and fellowship before school on Wednesdays.

Bryce's grin grew. "And be ready to stomp Paul and Marlys in that practice debate after school."

"Yeah, right!" Paul punched Bryce's shoulder and Marlys snickered, giving Katy a head-to-toes-and-up-again look that stirred Katy's irritation.

"I'll be ready," Katy vowed. Vengeful thoughts weren't encouraged by her Mennonite fellowship, but she couldn't deny hoping she and Bryce would beat Marlys and Paul.

Cold air smacked her bare legs as she headed toward the bus, which waited at the curb to transport students who stayed late for various activities. The temperature had dropped twenty degrees since Thanksgiving a week earlier, but so far no sign of snow. She shivered, envious of Marlys's and Vicki's warm denim jeans. Maybe she'd start wearing tights instead of her anklets even though the tights made her look like an old woman.

A car horn blared, and she spun toward the sound. Dad's pickup sat in the parking lot. She pulled her coat snug across her chest and dashed to the pickup. The warm air from the heater engulfed her as she climbed into the cab, and she let out a contented sigh. "Oooh, that feels good ..." She shot Dad a smile. "How come you're in town?"

Dad seldom picked her up from school. Their dairy farm outside of the little town of Schellberg was twelve miles from Salina. Dad didn't have time to take her back and forth to school. He had told her when she was given approval by the elders to attend public high school—the only student from her town ever to continue past ninth grade—that she'd have to ride the bus. She enjoyed those rare occasions when Dad drove her home instead of having to bounce down the highway in the noisy, crowded school bus.

Dad aimed the truck toward the street. "I needed to go to Wal-Mart for oil and a filter for the truck. I thought you might need some things too."

Katy couldn't think of anything she needed, except maybe a book on Looney Tunes characters. She wanted to look up the Tasmanian Devil. But she wouldn't tell Dad that.

"All I need is your signature," she said. She explained the upcoming debate trip and her chance to substitute for Vicki.

Dad listened attentively. When she finished sharing the details, he nodded. "That will be fine, Katy-girl. I'll sign it when we get home."

Katy grinned. "Thanks, Dad!" Dad circled the large Wal-Mart parking lot, seeking a spot close to the door. She gave him a hopeful look. "Can I pick up one of those cook-it-at-home pizzas from the deli? It'll be suppertime already when we get home."

Dad pulled his lips to the side, his expression dubious. "They're not as good as Aunt Rebecca's homemade pizzas, but they're not bad. I've had them at Shelby's house before. And it'll be a really quick thing to fix so you can get to milking the cows." Katy knew the cows would grow uncomfortable if the milking was delayed. Dad took good care of his dairy herd — he wouldn't want to leave them waiting for long.

"We won't need the pizza, Katy. Supper's ..." Pink filled Dad's cheeks.

Dread gnawed at the edges of Katy's mind. Dad only blushed over one thing. Or one *person*. "Supper's what?" She held her breath.

"Taken care of." Dad slid out of the truck without looking at Katy. "Mrs. Graber is bringing out a casserole and eating with us tonight."

Chapter Two

Katy's breath whooshed out. "Not *her* again ..." She hadn't meant to say it out loud.

Dad scowled. "Katy ..." He slammed his truck door and headed toward the store.

She'd already blurted her thoughts. She might as well continue. Scrambling out of the truck, she caught up to Dad and trotted alongside him. "I'm sorry. I didn't mean to be rude. But why is she bringing us supper? That's the third time since she came to visit Gramma Ruthie and Grampa Ben. Does she think I don't know how to cook?"

Dad released a snort of laughter. "Of course she doesn't question your ability to cook, Katy. She's just trying to be helpful."

Was Dad defending Mrs. Graber? She stepped into his path and folded her arms over her chest to keep from shivering. "She's been with Gramma and Grampa for a whole month now. Isn't she about ready to go home?"

Dad's scowl deepened. He tugged the brim of his ball cap lower on his forehead. "Her schedule isn't your concern, Katy. Your grandparents have told her she can stay for as long as she wants to." He put his fist on his hip. "And to be perfectly honest, I'm tired of you making her feel unwelcome."

Katy gawked at her dad. "I haven't done anything to her!" Dad's eyebrows rose. So did Katy's irritation. "Well, I *haven't*."

"No, but you sure haven't done anything to make her feel like she's part of our community."

She isn't part of our community. She just showed up, uninvited. Katy knew her thoughts weren't quite true. Gramma Ruthie had invited Mrs. Graber to come to Schellberg. And Katy knew why. She just didn't like the reason why.

Dad pointed at Katy. "When she comes over this evening, I expect you to be polite and friendly." He bobbed his head toward the double doors of the store. "Let's get in out of the cold."

Katy didn't move. "I don't need anything. I'm going back to the truck."

Dad shrugged. "Suit yourself." He strode off without her.

Katy let out a loud huff. Her breath hung in a little cloud in front of her face for a moment and then disappeared. She wished Mrs. Graber would disappear the same way. She stomped to the truck and slammed herself inside the cab.

She loved Gramma Ruthie with a fierce love. Gramma was the only mother Katy had ever known — her real mom had chosen to leave the Mennonite faith when Katy was four years old and had died in a car accident four years later. Katy couldn't love Gramma more if she tried. But lately Katy had been plenty frustrated with her grandmother.

From the very day Rosemary Graber arrived in Schellberg, Gramma had pushed Mrs. Graber and Dad at each other. Katy didn't *dislike* Mrs. Graber — she was a nice woman. But Gramma shouldn't play matchmaker. Especially not with a woman from another community. Katy's mother had come from Iowa to marry Dad, and she hadn't stayed. What if Mrs. Graber decided she didn't like Schellberg, either? How would Dad handle losing yet another wife? And how would Katy handle losing another mother?

Katy glared out the window, watching for Dad. "As if we need Mrs. Graber coming over and cooking for us and acting all sweet and helpful ..." Her breath steamed the window, and she swished the moisture away with her hand. It was cold in the truck. She wished Dad would hurry up.

Settling back into the seat, she hugged herself. Her stomach growled, and she hugged herself harder. No matter how wonderful Mrs. Graber's casserole looked, she wouldn't eat much. No sense in giving that smiley, capable woman any encouragement. Katy huffed again. Why couldn't Dad see that he and Katy were just fine on their own?

Guilt fell over her just like a damp sheet. *He's courting her because of me.* A few weeks ago Katy had gotten into trouble at school, and Dad had relied on Gramma Ruthie's help to deal with the problem. She heard his voice in her head — a comment he hadn't meant for her to hear: *"Katy needs a mother."*

If she hadn't gotten into trouble, Gramma Ruthie wouldn't have gone looking for someone to step in to be Katy's new mother. That meant it was up to Katy to convince Mrs. Graber she wasn't needed — or wanted — by Katy Lambright or her father.

"That was delicious, Rosemary." Dad wiped his mouth and smiled at Mrs. Graber. He looked at Katy. "Just as good as Gramma Ruthie's, wasn't it?"

It should be. It's her recipe. Katy swallowed the comment and forced a smile. "Very good, Mrs. Graber. Thank you." She poked at the mound of food on her plate. She'd barely eaten three bites of the cheesy chicken and cornbread stuffing casserole. Listening to Dad and Mrs. Graber talk and laugh like old friends during dinner had ruined her appetite. And she couldn't help but think Gramma Ruthie had purposely shared Dad's favorite casserole recipe with Mrs. Graber so the woman could score points with Dad.

"You're welcome." Mrs. Graber smiled sweetly. Her eyes crinkled at the corners. She had more lines on her face than Dad. But she smiled a lot more than Dad — although Dad seemed to wear a goofy grin whenever Mrs. Graber was around.

Katy jumped up. "I'll clear the dishes and get them washed. I'm sure you'll want to head back into town soon."

"Katy ..." Dad pushed her name through clenched teeth.

Katy sent him an innocent look.

Mrs. Graber laughed. "It has been a long day. But a good one." Her smile bounced back and forth between Katy and Dad. "Several of the town ladies and I spent the afternoon working on a quilt for next year's Mennonite Relief Sale. I love to quilt, but my arms are tired." She rose and began stacking plates and cups. "Let me help you, Kathleen. Don't you have homework?"

Katy considered allowing Mrs. Graber to do the dishes. For years, Katy had washed the breakfast, lunch, and supper dishes by hand because they didn't have an automatic dishwasher like the one in her friend Shelby's kitchen in Salina. What a treat to be released from that chore! But if Mrs. Graber washed them once, she might think she was welcome at Katy's sink, in Katy's kitchen, in Katy's life.

"Oh, no." Katy plucked the stack from Mrs. Graber's hands and forced a smile. "Your hands are tired from quilting. And dishwashing is one of my favorite duties. I'm happy to do it."

Dad shot Katy a startled look. She'd just lied, and Dad knew it. She pushed down the prickle of guilt in her chest and bounded to the sink, still jabbering. "Besides, you cooked supper. It's hardly fair to make you cook *and* clean up." Of course, Katy cooked and cleaned up every day, just like every other homemaker in Schellberg. She'd need to find a better argument. Whirling from the sink, she crowed, "And how silly would it be for you to do the cleanup in *my* kitchen? You don't know where the plates and cups and everything else belong in *my* cupboards. It's better if I just do it myself."

Dad now gawked at Katy, his face a mix of irritation and disbelief. But Mrs. Graber offered a nod and a soft laugh. "I'm sure you're right, Kathleen. It's best to allow you to manage your own kitchen." She turned to face Dad. "Since Kathleen has everything under control, Samuel, I believe I'll head back into town."

Katy heaved a huge sigh of relief. Finally, that woman was leaving!

Dad rose from the table. "I'll walk you to your car."

Katy rolled her eyes. Was Mrs. Graber incapable of finding her own car? It was parked right out by the barn!

"Thank you." Mrs. Graber reached for her coat, but Dad took it from the hook by the door and held it out for her. Katy tried hard not to watch while Mrs. Graber slipped her arms into the sleeves and Dad smoothed the blue wool over her shoulders. She didn't want to see Mrs. Graber's soft smile of thanks and Dad's grin in reply. But she couldn't look away. Her heart pounded fiercely against her ribs. Dad shouldn't get so close to that woman.

Dad opened the back door, and cool wind whisked into the kitchen. "Are you still open to going into Salina Friday evening for — " His voice faded away as he followed Mrs. Graber out of the house. The door banged shut behind them.

Katy leaned across the sink, pressed her forehead to the cold glass, and squinted out the window. Dusk had fallen while they ate, but she saw their two shadowy figures move side by side, their feet in perfect synchronization, across the gray yard. Then Dad's form stepped free of Mrs. Graber's, and his hand reached out to open the car door. The dome light sent out a meager glow as Mrs. Graber slid into the seat. But Dad didn't step away from the car. Instead, he leaned forward, sticking his head inside the car.

Pressing her fingertips to the glass, Katy stared, unblinking. What was he doing, leaning in there? Talking? Or could he be kissing that woman good-night? She held her breath, waiting for Dad to back out, but he didn't

24

emerge. With a gasp, she raced across the kitchen and threw open the back door. "Dad!"

Dad jerked upright and banged the back of his head on the car door opening. He rubbed his head and turned toward the house. "What?" He didn't sound happy.

What should she say? She couldn't ask what he was doing—it really wasn't her business. Her mind raced for a reason to have hollered. "When are you coming in?"

He balled his fist on his hip. He'd been doing that a lot lately. "Why?"

"Well ... um ... it's cold out there."

"Then stay inside." He leaned into the car again.

Katy slammed the door. She couldn't watch any longer. Her stomach churned. She just knew Dad was kissing that woman. *Kissing* her! And they had plans to go into Salina Friday night for ... something.

She ran water and clanked dishes around in the sink, her worry making her clumsy. Whatever Dad and Mrs. Graber had planned, she had to stop it. They were way too friendly. Things were moving way too fast. Somehow, she'd have to keep Dad home Friday. She'd have to get sick, or get hurt, or—

"Oh no!" She slapped a sudsy hand to her cheek. How could she keep Dad home when she wouldn't even be here? She'd be in Dodge City at the debate tournament. Gloom slumped her over the sink. What would she do now?

Chapter Three

Katy glanced at Dad when he stepped through the back door. He closed it with a firm click then placed his fist on his hip. *He'll give himself a callous there if he doesn't quit using his hip as a prop for his fist.*

"Katy-girl, we need to talk."

We sure do. Katy lifted a soapy plate from the sink and rinsed it. "About what?"

"Don't play innocent with me. You know about what."

Yep. Her. "I have homework, Dad. Can it wait until tomorrow?" She scrubbed a plate so hard she risked rubbing a hole right through it.

Dad clomped to the edge of the sink and folded his arms over his chest. His dark frown threatened to singe the ribbons on her cap. "Dry your hands, and look at me." The command came out in a low tone Dad rarely used.

Katy sucked in a breath and held it, her stomach quivering. She carefully dried her hands on the tea towel and shifted to face him. But she looked at Dad's unsmiling lips rather than into his eyes.

"Tell me why you dislike Mrs. Graber."

Katy's gaze jerked to meet Dad's. "I don't dislike her." She'd been honest. She didn't dislike Mrs. Graber. But neither did she like her. And she didn't want Dad to like her. Certainly not enough to kiss her!

"Then why are you rude to her?"

Katy sighed. Why couldn't Dad understand they didn't need this woman in their lives? "I'm not trying to be rude. I'm just ..." Katy licked her lips, searching for a reason her dad would accept. "She's here to visit you. Why do I have to talk to her?"

"For the same reason I talk to your friends when they come over."

Katy resisted rolling her eyes. Most of the time when she had friends over — which wasn't often — Dad hid out in the barn to avoid talking to them. He wasn't comfortable talking to her friends. She said, "But you don't."

Dad's eyebrows formed a stern V. "I don't what?"

"Talk to my friends."

The V deepened. "Yes, I do."

Some stubborn imp rose up inside Katy and nudged her. "No, you don't. You go out to the barn, or you read your newspaper. I entertain my friends. And that's fine. It's the way it should be." Katy gained steam, her words pouring out louder and faster. "They're my friends, not yours. It would be weird for you to want to spend time with them. So why should I — "

"Katy!" Dad ran his hand over his face. He looked very tired. "We aren't talking about me and your friends. We're talking about you and Mrs. Graber."

Katy swallowed. Her fingers twitched to finish the

dishwashing so she could escape to her bedroom. "What about her?"

Dad's shoulders rose and fell in a huge sigh. "I can see you're determined to be difficult."

Yep, I am. Where she's concerned, I really am.

Dad continued. "To be honest, I considered grounding you for the weekend after the way you behaved this evening during supper. But that would create a problem for your debate coach, so I'm not going to. But ..." Dad aimed his finger at Katy's nose. "The next time Mrs. Graber is a guest in our home, you will treat her with courtesy. You will answer her questions politely and will participate in conversation so she doesn't feel as if you're ignoring her."

Had Mrs. Graber complained to Dad about Katy? The question created an unpleasant taste in Katy's mouth. She wanted to spit it out, but Dad went on.

"Furthermore, if she offers assistance, you'll accept it graciously. And you won't try to rush her out the door. If she wants to stay and visit, she should feel comfortable doing so."

Katy jumped in defensively. "Dad, I only told her I could do my own dishes! And how could she have known where to put everything away? This is *my* kitchen." She almost choked on the words.

Dad shook his head. "You're missing the point. Deliberately, I'm sure." Dad leaned forward. "Katy, be nice. Rosemary is a kind, generous, godly woman. She doesn't deserve your discourtesy." He straightened. Pink streaked his face, but he looked Katy square in the eyes. "I intend to ask permission of the deacons to court her."

Katy gulped.

"If things go well, we'll be married at the end of February."

Katy's knees began to quake.

"So you're going to have to learn to get along with her. You might as well start now." Dad strode from the room.

Katy turned slowly and went back to washing dishes. The water was tepid, the scented suds a murky smear across the water's surface. Her chest ached. Dad officially courting Mrs. Graber? *Marrying* Mrs. Graber? Then that meant the woman would move into Katy's house. Be Dad's wife. Be Katy's mother.

Tears stung behind Katy's nose. She drained the unpleasant water and refilled the sink to finish the dishes. She hurried, eager to complete the task so she could run up to her room, shut herself away, and pour her thoughts into her journal. They wouldn't be good thoughts. She'd probably have to tear the paper to shreds and stuff the pieces into the wood-burning stove so no one would ever glimpse even a smidgen of the words running through her mind. But if she didn't put them on paper, they'd explode out of her mouth. And then she'd really be in trouble.

"Hey, Katy." Bryce tapped Katy's shoulder. She turned sideways in the van's middle seat to peer back at him. "How about we do a practice debate on the way to Dodge City?" He used his fist to bump Paul, who sat slumped in his seat with one knee raised. "You and me against Paul and Marlys — one final run before the real deal."

Paul dropped his foot and sat up eagerly. "Yeah! You could use the practice. So could Marlys."

Marlys huffed and spun to shoot a glare into the back-seat. "Like you couldn't!"

Paul laughed and flipped Marlys's hair over her face. "Just messin' with you. We know we rock." He held up his fist, and Marlys bumped her fist against it. They grinned at each other.

Katy shook her head. Sometimes Paul and Marlys sparred like enemies; other times, they acted like best friends. She couldn't figure them out. But she supposed it didn't matter. "I don't mind practicing again."

After yesterday afternoon's practice, Mr. Gorsky had deemed her ready to compete. His confidence gave her confidence in herself, but Gramma Ruthie liked to say, "Practice makes perfect." Katy wanted to be at her very best for the tournament. Besides, practicing would get her mind off the fact that she wouldn't be home to prevent Dad from taking Mrs. Graber to Salina for dinner.

"Great!" Bryce dragged the debate briefcases from the storage area behind the seat and handed them out. "Let's not keep flow sheets. I get carsick if I try to write in a moving vehicle. We can just talk it through."

"Good thinking," Paul said, "'cause I don't want you spewing your guts out all over back here and hitting me."

Marlys laughed as if Paul had said something hilarious. Katy rolled her eyes.

"But we ought to trade places." Paul unhooked his seat belt. "I need to sit by Marlys, and you need to sit by Kathleen."

"Paul, stay put." Mr. Gorsky's eyes flitted to the rearview mirror. "No changing seats while the van's in motion. You can practice just fine without sitting beside your partner."

Katy sighed. She wouldn't have minded sitting beside Bryce. At least he talked to her. So far, the debate squad had managed to load their overnight bags and equipment, climb into the van, and drive several miles without Marlys so much as looking at Katy, let alone talking to her.

Katy listened to Paul present the affirmative plan, called the *prima facie* case—Katy relished the unique term— then Bryce questioned him. Marlys kept track of the time on her silver wristwatch, hollering, "Stop!" in place of flashing a red time card. Then it was Katy's turn to refute Paul's case. She noticed Mr. Gorsky's eyes flitting to the rearview mirror as she spoke, and she read his approval. The look boosted her confidence again, and her voice rose with fervor as she defended the present system.

Time flew quickly as they continued with Paul and Marlys as the affirmative team then switched to allow Bryce and Katy time to present their plan for building greener prison facilities. Katy didn't particularly care for the plan—the idea that prisons were needed made her uncomfortable—but as a substitute, she didn't have any choice in the matter. She had to try to convince the judge of the sensibility of the plan.

Being enthusiastic about something that didn't thrill her taxed her acting abilities, but when they finished, Mr. Gorsky called from the front seat, "Good job! Quick assessment. Bryce, check your research concerning the energy source. I think you may have misrepresented how many watts of power can be pulled from one wind turbine."

Bryce immediately began riffling through his notes.

"Paul, remember to watch the tone you use. Try not to sneer."

Paul twisted his face into a mock snarl. Marlys giggled.

"Marlys, during cross-examination, don't be afraid to push a little harder. Rattle your opponent."

Marlys leaned forward, holding out her hands in silent protest. "I'm trying to go easy on poor Kathleen here."

"You don't need to go easy on Kathleen." Mr. Gorsky flashed an encouraging smile in the rearview mirror. "Kathleen, you get better every time. Hold your ground. I think you're going to do well at the tournament. Now, get some rest. We'll have two rounds this evening, and you'll need your energy."

"Sure thing, Mr. G," Paul said. Bryce flipped the briefcases back into the storage area, and the two boys leaned into opposite corners. Marlys flopped back into the seat with her arms crossed and closed her eyes. Katy wriggled into the corner and tried to relax, but excitement kept her alert and restless for the remainder of the drive.

When they reached Dodge City, Mr. Gorsky parked beside a row of vans and buses from several schools. He turned off the ignition, and Bryce, Paul, and Marlys came to life. They bounced out of the van. Katy quickly followed. Mr. Gorsky met them at the rear of the van and began handing out their cases of research materials and briefcases. Katy's hands trembled as she caught hold of Vicki's case.

Mr. Gorsky frowned. "Are you all right?"

Her stomach turned cartwheels. "I'm okay. It's just kind of cold out here."

The teacher nodded. "Well then, let's hurry and get inside."

Katy trailed behind the others, but Bryce slowed his steps and fell in beside her. He shot her a grin. "Nervous?"

Katy hunched her shoulders. "I think so." Either that or she was coming down with the flu. Her stomach didn't feel right at all.

"Don't worry." Bryce brushed against her with his elbow. By accident or on purpose? She hoped he'd done it on purpose, even though the thought made her stomach turn another swirl. "I'm always nervous right before I start a round, but once we get going, I forget all about it because I'm so caught up in the challenge. It'll be that way for you too. You'll see."

Katy hoped he was right. On her first day of school at Salina High North, she'd had to run to the bathroom to throw up. She didn't want to do that her first day of debating. Bryce was depending on her as his partner. She couldn't let him — or Mr. Gorsky — down.

Mr. Gorsky directed them to the cafeteria where all of the teams huddled in little groups while waiting for the rounds to start. "I'll go register you and get your team numbers. Wait here."

Katy glanced around at the various groups, her pulse skipping at twice its regular pace. She twirled a ribbon from her cap around her finger. The boys all wore shirts and ties. Some wore suits. The girls wore skirts and jackets or suits similar to ones worn by the boys, only with high-heeled, girly shoes. She smoothed the skirt of her best dress and glanced down at her black oxfords. At least she'd put on pantyhose instead of anklets, but her clothes still stuck out.

She noticed a few people looking at her in curiosity. Even though she was used to people staring at her clothes, she didn't like it. She turned her back on the room, and her gaze collided with Marlys's bold fuchsia skirt and jacket with quarter-sized black buttons. She bit down on her lower lip. She even stuck out with her own teammates. So far Bryce hadn't seemed to care that she dressed differently — but now that they were away from Salina and mixing with kids from other schools, would he be embarrassed to be seen with her? Clutching her hands at her waist, she wished Dad would let her wear a suit like the other girls. Just for tournaments.

Mr. Gorsky approached at a brisk pace, carrying a large yellow envelope. He opened it, flipped through the pages, and distributed their schedules. She scanned the paper. She and Bryce were team 4B, and they'd start in room 312.

Bryce traced his finger on the map provided by the tournament coordinators. "Okay, here's where we go." He grinned teasingly. "Look. It's right next to the bathrooms, so we're good."

Katy's ears burned hot, and she sent up a silent prayer that she wouldn't need to escape to the bathroom. Suddenly, she realized she was overly warm, and so she unbuttoned her sweater. Just as she removed it, the loudspeaker clicked on, and an announcement blared.

"All debaters, make your way to your first round locations. Round One will begin in five minutes."

Bryce pulled up the handle on his rolling case and flashed a bright smile. "This is it! Let's go."

Katy squared her shoulders. "I'm ready." But her stomach continued to churn.

Chapter Four

"You should have seen her."

Katy hunched her shoulders and giggled as Bryce paused in eating and launched into a description of her cross-examination during their final round of the day. The first round had gone so smoothly, her stomach hadn't even bothered her during the second round. She'd been able to fully focus on debating. And it had been fun!

Bryce stabbed his fork into his baked potato and shook his head. "There she stood, looking all innocent but firing off question after question with hardly a breath in between. She had the kid squirming in his pants!"

Katy squirmed in her own seat, her ears warming. Usually, when her ears grew hot, it meant she was embarrassed or irritated ... usually because of Caleb Penner. But getting flustered over Bryce's praise was a good feeling.

Paul laughed. "Huh! Who'd have guessed? Kathleen a tiger." He pointed his steak knife at her. "Maybe we'll have to pair up sometime — could be interesting."

Marlys shot a glare at Paul, and Katy quickly said, "Oh,

that's all right. I'll stay with Bryce." Marlys's lips twitched, but she didn't say anything.

Mr. Gorsky said, "All of you did well today. I stopped by the tab room and checked our record. Right now, as a team we're up three to one, with sixteen speaker points."

Bryce and Paul did a double high-five and Marlys crowed, "Ooo, snap!" Katy remained silent, but pleasure zinged through her middle. Although she still found the speaker point system a bit confusing, she knew three to one meant they'd won three rounds and lost only one. Winning more than losing was a good thing.

Paul paused with his knife and fork over his steak. "So what about Marlys and me? How many of those wins are ours?"

Mr. Gorsky shook his head. "Nope. You know better than to ask. We're here as a team. You'll get your individual stats at the end of the tournament."

Paul shrugged and began cutting into his steak with his elbows high. "Think about it, though." He flashed a knowing look around the table. "If we do that well tomorrow, we could be one of the trophy winners."

Katy gasped. Wouldn't that be something? Her first tournament, and to come home with a trophy!

"It's possible," Mr. Gorsky confirmed, "but don't get overconfident. It can affect your performance."

"Sure thing, Mr. G." Paul popped a piece of steak into his mouth and spoke around it. "I'll be givin' my all tomorrow. And so will everybody else, right?"

Katy added her "Right!" to the chorus, and then she focused on her meal. She was surprisingly hungry, considering her uneasy stomach earlier in the day. The chicken-fried steak and mashed potatoes weren't as good as Gramma Ruthie's—the potatoes had a funny flavor and a gritty texture—but Katy ate everything on her plate. The school paid for it, so she wouldn't be wasteful.

After dinner, Mr. Gorsky drove the team to the hotel where they'd spend the night. As she suspected, she and Marlys would share a room. When Mr. Gorsky held out the room card, Marlys snatched it from his hand without giving Katy an opportunity to take it. Then she charged toward the elevators without a backward glance.

With a little jerk, Katy grabbed her small overnight bag and trotted after her. They rode in silence to the third floor, and Katy followed Marlys to a door on the left. Marlys swiped the card through a slot, a little green light flashed, and she swung open the door. Only then did she glance back and acknowledge Katy's presence.

"I want the bed closest to the bathroom."

Katy didn't care. She nodded and plopped her bag on the bed near the window. Marlys disappeared into the bathroom, and Katy turned a slow circle, admiring the room. Ceiling-to-floor draperies in a bold geometric print matched the bedspreads. Each bed held four big, plump pillows. She could create a nest if she wanted to. A large painting of a field of flowers hung above her bed, reflected in a huge mirror across the room. A dresser, tall cabinet, and a desk stood in a line facing the beds. Although the room was a bit crowded with all of the furnishings, it felt cozy rather than cluttered.

She looked down at the wall-to-wall carpeting and, without hesitation, sat on the edge of the bed and pulled off her shoes. Then she ran her soles over the plush, light brown carpet. It was like walking barefoot on thick moss. She giggled.

Marlys zipped around the corner and caught her. Her lips formed a snide grin. "Don't tell me—you've never stayed in a hotel before."

Katy bounced up, clasping her hands in front of her. She shook her head, making the ribbons on her cap dance.

"Well, as far as accommodations go, this is hardly first-class." Marlys gave the room a quick, unsmiling perusal. "But it's only one night, so I'll survive." She tugged at the hem of her lime green pajama top. "Bathroom's open—change if you want to. I'll shower in the morning."

Katy usually took her bath at bedtime, so she grabbed her bag and scuttled into the bathroom. For a moment she gawked at the sleek, floating countertop that stretched from one side of the bathroom to the other and the mirror that rose clear to the ceiling. She couldn't resist running her fingers along the smooth, speckled top of the counter, so different from the simple pedestal sink in her bathroom at home.

Then, realizing she was wasting time, she gave herself a little shake and ran the bathwater. A half hour later, she slipped into her cotton nightgown and brushed out her hair. Then, with her damp hair trailing down her back in a loose braid, she joined Marlys. The other girl lounged on her bed, propped up by a pile of pillows, including one from Katy's bed. The door of the tall cabinet stood open, revealing a television set, which mumbled softly into the room.

Katy averted her gaze as she quickly darted past the television set. She needed to tell Marlys that she wasn't allowed to watch television, but she sensed Marlys wouldn't really care about Katy's rules. She might be a debater now, but she had no desire to debate with Marlys. So she threw the covers back and curled up on her side on the bed, keeping the television behind her and out of sight.

After a moment, Marlys said, "You going to sleep? 'Cause I can turn the TV down if it bothers you."

Surprised by Marlys's consideration, Katy admitted, "I'm not really sleepy."

"Then sit up and watch. This show is a rerun, but it's pretty good."

Katy didn't budge. "I—I can't."

"Can't what? Sit up?" Sarcasm laced Marlys's words.

Katy sucked on a breath. "No, I can't watch television. I'm not supposed to. My dad wouldn't be pleased." For several seconds, Katy waited for Marlys to reply. Marlys didn't say a word, but suddenly the television fell silent. Katy shifted slightly to peek over her shoulder. Marlys had her arms crossed, but she met Katy's gaze and she didn't appear too upset.

"Okay, it's off. Go ahead and sit up."

Katy scooted into a sitting position and leaned against the pillows. Her nightgown rode up above her knees, and she smoothed it back to mid-calf. Marlys watched, one eye-brow raised. Katy could imagine what the other girl was thinking. Her ears felt hot. To make amends, she said, "I'm sorry you had to turn it off."

Marlys yawned and ran her hands through her hair. "No biggie. Like I said, it was a rerun." She scrunched her brow and looked across the room toward Katy. "But what do you do all evening if you don't watch TV?"

Katy shrugged slowly. "My chores, my homework,

read . . ." Saying it all out loud made it sound terribly boring. She wanted to turn the focus back on Marlys. "Do you watch a lot of TV?"

"Yeah." Marlys lifted the covers with her feet and then snuggled underneath. "It's either that or listen to my mom and stepdad fight."

"What do they fight about?" Katy blurted the question without thinking. It was nosy. She should have held it inside.

But Marlys laughed, so she couldn't have been offended. "Mostly me." She grinned. "But I bet you don't have that problem, do you? Fighting is probably against the rules."

Katy didn't know that it was against the rules, but her Mennonite sect tried to practice peaceful resolution. She said, "No, we don't fight much. But then, it's just Dad and me." They'd never fought much. *Until Mrs. Graber came along . . .*

Marlys wriggled into her pillows. "Well, for my whole life, off and on, it's been Mom, my brother, and me. And we find plenty to fight about. It's kind of nice when Mom marries, 'cause then she fights with somebody else for a while." She snorted. "Believe it or not, I'm on my third stepfather and my second stepmother since my folks divorced. You could say I'm a pro at fighting."

Katy pressed her palms to the mattress and sat straight up. "You have a stepmother?"

Marlys huffed. "Yeah. I just said that."

"Do you like her?"

"Better than the last one. She didn't even last a year." A sly smile crept up Marlys's cheek. "It didn't take my brother and me long to run her off."

Katy's heart began to pound. She licked her lips. Marlys hadn't minded her last prying question, so Katy braved a second one. "How'd you do it?"

Marlys tipped her head, another sly smile creasing her cheek. "You really wanna know?"

Katy nodded eagerly. If there was a way to get rid of Mrs. Graber before she became Katy's stepmother, then nothing would have to change.

Marlys laughed. "It's really not too tough. It just takes acting — and a little bit of sneakiness."

"Sneakiness?" A Bible verse from Hebrews skipped through Katy's mind. *Pray for us: for we trust we have a good conscience, in all things willing to live honestly.* Being sneaky wasn't exactly honest. But if it would save Dad from making a big mistake, surely it would be worth it.

"Yeah. My brother and I call it 'The Brat Plan.' See ..." Marlys flipped to her side and leaned on her elbow. "Whenever you're with both your dad and your stepmom, you act all sweet and cooperative. This gets the stepmom to relax, thinking she's won you over. Then when your dad's not around, you do the exact opposite. Talk back, refuse to do anything she asks, just be a total brat."

Marlys pointed at Katy, her expression serious. "But *never* do it where your dad can see or hear. 'Cause what you want is for your stepmom to complain to your dad — to accuse you of being bratty. He might ask you about it, but since he's never seen it, all you have to do is act all innocent and hurt. Then he'll defend you, and it'll drive a wedge between them. Before long ..." Marlys flopped back against the pillows. "They've split. She blames you, but he blames her. It's perfect."

"That really works?" Katy couldn't hide her skepticism. Adults really fell for a trick like that?

Marlys grinned. "Oh, yeah, like a charm. I've gotten rid of one stepmom and two stepdads that way. And what's even better, last time my mom felt so bad about me and my brother being so misunderstood, she bought a brand-new CD stereo for the family room." She nodded, her smile wide. "Doesn't get any better than that."

She glanced at the clock on the table between the beds. "Oh, wow, look at the time. We have to be downstairs ready to go by seven fifteen in the morning. We better get some sleep." Without waiting for Katy's reply, she snapped off the lamp above her bed, plunging the room into darkness.

Katy listened to Marlys rooting around in the bed for a little while, then her deep breathing indicated she'd fallen asleep. But Katy couldn't sleep. Unfamiliar noises — thuds and voices from the hallway, a drip-drip from the bathroom faucet, and traffic sounds from outside — intruded, keeping her from relaxing. And her mind refused to shut down.

She kept replaying Marlys's advice. Although Marlys's "brat plan" wasn't an option — the last person she'd want to emulate was Marlys Horton! — there had to be a way to make Mrs. Graber go back to Meschke, Kansas, where she belonged. If she could only think of one ...

Chapter Five

"Can I hold it now?" Katy looked with longing into the backseat, where the trophy was propped in Paul's lap. He hadn't released it since the tournament's coordinator placed it in his hands during the awards ceremony at the end of the tournament.

With an impish grin, Paul hugged the trophy to his chest. "Oh, no. It's mine. All mine."

Marlys whirled around. "And why is it all yours?"

"If it hadn't been for my great speaker points, we would've lost this puppy to Skyline."

Bryce and Marlys groaned, and Katy joined in. In wins and losses, their team had tied with a Pratt team, both winning nine and losing three rounds. But Katy's team had one less speaker point, which gave them the lead.

Mr. Gorsky angled the van onto the highway for the return trip home. "Now, Paul, we could also say that if any of the others had fallen into one lower position, the trophy would have gone to Skyline. Those points were earned jointly. I think you're giving yourself too much credit."

"Aw, c'mon, Mr. G, that's harsh." Paul faked a quick

pout. Then he cradled the trophy in his palms and held it toward Katy. "All right then, go ahead and hold it for a minute or two. But don't smudge it up with your fingers. I want that little brass plaque nice and shiny when we get back to school."

Katy lifted the trophy over the seat and rested it on her knee. She smiled at the brass plate that read THIRD PLACE—SOUTHWEST KANSAS—NOVICE DEBATERS TOURNAMENT—DODGE CITY, KANSAS. Later, Mr. Gorsky had said, the school would imprint each of their names in smaller letters beneath the heading. She envisioned her name—KATHLEEN LAMBRIGHT—there with Paul Andress, Marlys Horton, and Bryce Porter. Alphabetically, she'd fall between Marlys and Bryce with Paul at the top. She stifled a giggle. Paul would probably change his name if it didn't already start with the first letter of the alphabet.

"So how does it feel to be an award-winning debater?" Mr. Gorsky asked the question, his eyes meeting Katy's in the rearview mirror.

Katy closed her eyes, savoring the moment. "It feels great." She couldn't wait to tell her friends Shelby, Cora, Trisha, Bridget, and Jewel. Jewel especially. Jewel had laughed when she found out Katy wanted to join the debate squad. Jewel would be more surprised than anyone at how well Katy had done. Although she and Bryce had won four rounds overall, one fewer than Paul and Marlys, Mr. Gorsky had assured her she'd done *exemplarily*—yet another word to savor—for her first competition.

She smoothed her finger over the brass figure at the top of the trophy, remembering how it felt to stand in front of the judges and passionately plead her case. She'd convinced them that she was right and the other team was wrong. The power was exhilarating. Her heart thudded as another thought wiggled through her brain: *If I have the power to convince a judge that I was in the right—a judge who didn't even know my real name—then how much more powerful could I be in convincing Dad, who's known me since birth, that we have no need of Mrs. Graber in our lives?*

"All right, Kathleen, you've held it long enough." Marlys's demanding voice cut into Katy's thoughts. She reached for the trophy, wiggling her fingers. "Hand it over."

With a reluctant sigh, Katy relinquished the trophy to Marlys's hands. The van rolled down the highway toward home, and Katy's mind rolled through what Marlys had shared in their hotel room. This tournament win had given her the confidence to use her persuasive skills in a much more personal matter. She'd found her plan.

"You're not serious."

Annika's disbelieving tone made Katy's resolve waver for a moment, but then she grabbed her friend's arm and tugged her behind the church building. It was cold on the shaded side of the church, but no one would overhear them from here. Katy hissed fervently, "I am very serious. Making logical arguments convinces a judge that you're right. Why shouldn't it work for me with my dad?"

"Katy, didn't your dad decide to start courting because he thought you needed a mother?"

Katy bit down on her lower lip. How could she forget that day last fall when Dad, Gramma Ruthie, and Grampa Ben all talked to her about making good choices at the public school? Dad didn't know she'd heard him say he needed to move on and find a new wife so Katy would have a mother. But the comment had haunted her. It also convinced her that he wasn't courting Mrs. Graber because he wanted to, but out of obligation to Katy. And that was all the more reason to send Mrs. Graber back to Meschke.

She said, "Yes, but I don't see what diff—"

"If you start arguing with him at every turn," Annika interrupted, "then won't he just think you really need a mother to settle you down?"

Katy nibbled the inside of her cheek. She hadn't considered Dad misinterpreting her arguments. But Annika didn't understand debate. "Debating isn't just random arguing. It means presenting logical arguments intended to sway the opposition to your way of thinking." She groaned. *How would she find enough words to convince Dad they were okay as they were?*

She slapped her forehead then grabbed Annika's arm. "Annika, it will work!"

"How do you know?"

"Dad started courting Mrs. Graber because he thinks a mother will help me make good decisions. If he sees me making good decisions even without Mrs. Graber's influence, then there won't be any need for him to court her, right?"

"But, Katy—"

"And if, while I'm proving with my behavior that I don't need a mother, I can grab every opportunity to keep them apart and show Dad how well we're doing without her. I'll debate with my *actions* as much as my words."

Annika frowned. "I don't know, Katy ..."

48

"I *do* know. It's the only way. So being extra good and extra helpful and extra sweet will tell Dad I'm just fine without a mom." She flipped her hands outward. "See? Problem solved."

"So what do you have against Mrs. Graber, anyway?" Annika tipped her head to the side. The white ribbon from her cap fluttered against her shoulder.

Katy stared at the quivering white ribbon and bit down on her lower lip. Truthfully, she didn't have anything against Mrs. Graber. Not directly. But the woman took away what little attention she received from her dad. Katy already competed with the cows. She didn't need another distraction. Annika wouldn't understand. She had a mom, dad, and several brothers and sisters at her house. All Katy had was Dad.

"We just don't need her," she said, stubbornly sticking out her chin.

Annika folded her arms over her chest and shivered. "I think bringing that debate stuff into your house and using it on your dad is proving that the worldly kids are affecting you. You better be careful, Katy."

Katy paused. Maybe she shouldn't have confided in Annika. But they were best friends — she counted on Annika supporting her. Maybe even helping her. But would Annika tattle instead? She'd done it before when she thought Katy was stepping outside the boundaries established for their Old Order fellowship. She grabbed Annika's elbow.

"You aren't going to tell anyone about my plan, are you?"

Annika crunched her lips together.

Katy's fingers twitched on Annika's arms. "Are you?"

Annika shook her head, and Katy nearly wilted with relief. But then Annika said, "I don't think I'll have to tell. I'm pretty sure your dad is smart enough to figure it out on his own."

Katy opened her mouth to argue, but a second voice intruded. An annoying voice.

"Hey, Katydid, there you are."

Katy spun around and scowled at Caleb Penner. "Stop calling me Katydid. I'm a girl, not a bug. And why're you following me?" Katy had never liked Caleb. He teased too much. And since he now worked for her dad in the dairy, she had to see him every day.

He shrugged, grinning like a fool. "Your dad sent me to find you. You're having lunch at our place today. My mom invited you, your grandparents, and Mrs. Graber." His gaze flicked to Annika. "Did you invite Antarctica to eat with you?"

Katy slipped her hand through Annika's elbow. "Most Sundays, we eat together."

Caleb heaved an exaggerated sigh. "Well, tell you what, Katydid. Mom'll say there's enough food to go around, so go ahead and bring Antarctica along too." He grinned and zipped around the corner.

"We better go," Annika said, "since your dad wants you, and you're going to be pulling this Miss Nice Girl act. You can't leave him waiting."

Katy ignored Annika's disapproving tone and followed her to the front churchyard. Dad leaned on the hood of his truck, and Mrs. Graber stood beside him. Close beside him. The now familiar irritation climbed like a spider up Katy's spine.

"Should I ask my mom if I can eat with you?" Annika asked.

Without looking at her friend, Katy said yes. She waited until Annika took off toward her parents' car, then she forced her lips into a smile and jogged across the ground to her dad. Although temptation to step between the two adults smacked her hard, she stopped a few feet away instead.

"Caleb said you're ready to go." She flashed the smile in Mrs. Graber's direction and kept her voice friendly, the way Dad had instructed her. "Mrs. Graber, were you planning to ride with Dad and me? We can sit three across in his pickup, but I have to warn you, it isn't very comfortable to straddle the gearshift."

Mrs. Graber laughed softly in return. "I suppose you're right."

Dad said, "Katy, since the gearshift is a problem for you, why don't you ride with your Gramma Ruthie and Grampa Ben? You don't get to see them much now since you're so busy with school. They'd probably enjoy the extra time with you."

Katy stared at Dad in dismay. He'd defeated her first argument without any effort at all. But he was right — she hardly ever saw Gramma Ruthie these days, and she missed her dear grandmother. With a start, she realized she'd probably see even less of Gramma Ruthie when Mrs. Graber moved in. Gramma would let Mrs. Graber help Katy with sewing projects and new recipes ...

Even though she didn't want to leave Dad and Mrs. Graber alone, she suddenly wanted time with Gramma. *Dad, 1 – Katy, 0.* "All right, Dad."

Katy spun and trotted toward her grandparents' sedan. When she reached it, she glanced over her shoulder and spotted Dad's hand curled around Mrs. Graber's elbow as he helped her into the truck. Jealousy tried to attack, but she pushed it aside. She had to be *pleasant*. Lifting her hand in a wave, she called, "'Bye, Dad! See you at the Penners'." Dad slammed the door behind Mrs. Graber and waved back.

Annika ambled up beside Katy. She gazed across the grounds until Dad's pickup roared to life and he pulled out of the parking area. Then she looked at Katy and shook her head. "What you're doing is just like lying. I'll go to the Penners' for lunch today, but don't ask me to play your game with you."

Katy hissed, "Shh!" She glanced around, relieved that Gramma Ruthie and Grampa Ben were caught up talking to another couple and didn't seem to hear what Annika had said. "I'm only doing it to keep Dad from making a big mistake."

"You're only doing it out of selfishness. And wrong behavior will never make a right."

Katy sighed. Why did Annika always make her feel guilty? Or was it her own conscience pricking her? "Get in the car," she said.

Chapter Six

Katy's acting abilities were put to the test during dinner at the Penners' place. Mrs. Penner had seated her between Annika and Caleb — a spot she wouldn't have chosen. Her location put her directly across the table from Dad and Mrs. Graber where she witnessed every exchanged glance and bump of elbows. She was sure some of those little bumps were deliberate. She had to force back growls of protest.

Plus, Caleb's manners left much to be desired. He stuck out his elbow when he cut his meat, nearly banging her in the nose more than once. Two different times he stretched his long arm across her plate to grab bowls of food. Couldn't he ask to have things passed? And he smacked his food. Katy had never been allowed to smack while chewing, and the sound set her teeth on edge. But no one at the table would have guessed her annoyance. Somehow she managed to smile and converse and behave as though she didn't have a care in the world.

When the serving dishes of simmered steak, mashed potatoes, green beans, carrots, and applesauce were finally empty, Mrs. Penner shot a wide smile around the table. "Is everyone ready for dessert? I baked Caleb's favorite, pine-apple upside-down cake."

Caleb grinned at Katy as if he'd done something special that required recognition. She offered a weak smile in return then picked up her napkin and busily wiped her mouth.

Grampa Ben patted his stomach. "Cake sounds good to me."

A murmur of agreements went around the table.

"Good, I'll bring it right out." Mrs. Penner turned toward the kitchen.

Mrs. Graber rose. "Let me help you."

Katy lurched to her feet. "Oh, don't bother, Mrs. Graber. I can give Mrs. Penner a hand. You stay and visit." She bounded after Caleb's mother, relieved to leave Caleb's presence even if it meant she couldn't keep an eye on Dad and Mrs. Graber.

In the kitchen, Mrs. Penner handed Katy a large knife and pointed to the cake on the counter. "Cut the cake into good-sized pieces, Katy, and use those serving plates stacked next to the sink. I'm going to whip up some cream."

Katy's ears tuned to the soft conversation and occasional bursts of laughter drifting from the dining room. It seemed Mrs. Graber was entertaining the others with a story about the time her daughter made pineapple upside-down cake and forgot the sugar. Katy pursed her lips, imagining the sour result. Eager to return to the dining room before Dad could tell any stories about her cooking fiascos, she plopped the last piece of cake on a plate and rinsed the knife in the sink.

"Do you have a tray to carry the dessert plates on?"
Katy didn't mind helping, but she didn't want to make a
half-dozen trips back and forth.

Mrs. Penner frowned, tapping her lip. "Yes. But I
haven't used it for a while. I can't remember ... Oh!" She
pointed. "Look in the cabinet above the refrigerator."

Katy turned toward the refrigerator, but she knew she
wouldn't be able to reach the cabinet doors. They were too
high. She glanced around for a step stool.

Mrs. Penner must have figured out Katy's dilemma,
because she called, "Caleb! Come in here for a minute,
please."

Caleb clomped into the kitchen, a foolish grin on his
face. "Yeah, Ma?"

"Katy needs the serving tray from above the refrigerator. Get it down for her, would you?"

"Sure thing." Caleb strutted forward importantly, forcing Katy to skitter backward or be run down. His long
arms stretched out and he plucked a square silver tray
from the cabinet. He offered it to Katy with a broad smile.
"Here you go, Katydid."

"Caleb ..." Mrs. Penner clicked her tongue on her teeth.
"Stop calling Katy that ridiculous nickname. You're going
to make an enemy of the girl."

Too late. He accomplished that at least three years ago.
Katy held the thought inside and took the tray from Caleb's
freckled hands. "Thanks." She turned her back on Caleb
and began arranging the dessert plates on the tray.

Mrs. Penner scooped the freshly whipped cream into a
bowl, added a spoon, and placed the bowl on the corner of
the tray. She lifted the tray from the counter and offered a

smile that reached clear to Katy's heart. "Thank you, dear. I appreciate your help."

Basking in the glow of Mrs. Penner's warm appreciation, Katy returned to the dining room and quickly cleared a spot on the table for the tray. She started to help serve, but Mrs. Penner waved her away with a light laugh. "No, you've done enough. Sit down. I'll serve."

Katy slid back into her seat, careful not to brush against Caleb. He sat with his legs widespread and his elbows on the table, leaving her very little space. If she ever came to his parents' house for a meal again, she'd insist on sitting across the table from the rude boy. *But then he'd probably be kicking me.*

Conversation stopped while everyone ate their dessert. The cake was moist and sweet, and Katy savored every bite even though it was Caleb's favorite.

Caleb pressed his fork tines against his plate, picking up the tiniest crumbs. He licked the fork clean then dropped it on his napkin. He pushed back his chair. "Dad, can the girls and me hitch up the old buggy and go for a drive?"

"The girls and *I*," Katy corrected without thinking.

Caleb sent her a puzzled look. "What?"

Katy flicked a glance around the table before facing Caleb again. "What you said—the girls and me—was grammatically incorrect. You wouldn't say, 'Can *me* go hitch up the old buggy,' would you? If you would use 'I' by itself, then you should use it when it's part of a compound subject, such as in 'the girls and I.'"

Caleb stared at her with his Adam's apple bobbing. Katy thought he looked like a bullfrog sucking air. Even though she hadn't meant to strike him silent, she admitted to being pleased by the result.

"Why, Kathleen . . ." Mrs. Graber's eyes widened in amazement. "That was an excellent explanation. You would make a very good teacher."

Katy shrugged, shooing away the pleasure the woman's words created. "Thank you, but I don't want to be a teacher. I want to be a writer."

Mrs. Graber opened her mouth to say something else, but Caleb blurted, "So can we, Dad?"

Katy held her breath. She had no desire to go buggy-riding with Caleb, but she couldn't refuse without looking uncooperative. And she couldn't be uncooperative today, not with her new plan in full swing.

"It's too cold for that today, Caleb. Even with a lap blanket, you kids would probably catch a chill," Mr. Penner answered.

Katy nearly melted with relief, but Caleb slumped in his chair. Annika, too, seemed to wilt with disappointment. Katy pasted on a bright smile. "Maybe another time. It'll warm up eventually, you know. Besides, Annika and I are going to do the dishes for your mom to say thank you for this wonderful meal."

Mrs. Penner said, "Now Katy —"

Katy bounced up. "Oh, we insist." She began stacking her dishes with Caleb's, who stared at her like she'd lost her mind.

"Are you sure?" Mrs. Penner sounded dubious.

"Of course!" Katy grinned. "If I were at home, I'd be washing dishes. So I don't mind at all. Really, I want to. You've been such a kind hostess. Besides, you grown-ups will want to sip coffee and visit, so we'll just get this mess out of your way."

Mrs. Penner laughed and shook her head. "All right, then. You heard Katy. I'll get a fresh pot of coffee, and we can go to the living room to visit."

Katy said, "Let us get that coffee." She risked a quick glance at Dad. Would he think she was being pushy? He'd never cared for impudence of any kind. His approving smile spurred her forward. "You just go relax. Annika and I have it all under control."

Mrs. Penner came around the table and gave each of the girls a quick hug. "Thank you, Katy and Annika. You've given me a sweet gift."

The adults headed to the living room. Katy tried not to stare when Dad put his hand on Mrs. Graber's back as they rounded the corner.

Caleb swung out of his chair and held up both hands. "Don't think *I'm* helping with dishes."

Katy wrinkled her nose at him. "Of course not. You'd just be in our way, right, Annika?"

Annika frowned and didn't answer.

"I'm going to my room." Caleb disappeared down the hallway. A door slammed a few seconds later.

Katy heaved a sigh of relief. "Finally! I thought he'd never leave."

Annika's scowl deepened. "I happen to enjoy Caleb's company, Katy, as you well know. And I don't know how *I* got stuck washing dishes. Part of the reason I like to go to someone else's house on Sunday is so I don't have to do dishes. So thanks a lot!" She snatched up a stack of plates and stomped into the kitchen.

Katy hurried after her. "Don't be mad, Annika. I'll do all the washing and drying. You can just talk to me, okay?"

Annika huffed.

Katy clasped her hands beneath her chin. "But would you make the pot of coffee and take it out to them?"

Annika rolled her eyes, but she lifted the coffeepot from the stove and carried it to the sink. While Annika prepared the coffee, Katy cleared the table. It took all the willpower she possessed to keep from peeking into the living room to find out if Dad and Mrs. Graber were sitting all cozy together on the sofa or if they'd chosen separate chairs. She replayed the time at the table. She'd been polite, cheerful, and helpful. Dad had smiled and nodded at her. Her chest expanded when she remembered the tenderness in his eyes. He was pleased with her behavior. She knew it. *Dad 1 – Katy 1.*

She ran sudsy water, humming to herself. Annika was mad, but she'd get over it. What mattered most was Dad didn't have any reason to complain. If Katy could keep it up, his whole notion of her needing a mom would fly right out the window. *So far, so good.*

Chapter Seven

Katy hunched into her coat while she waited for the morning bell to ring. She wished the school would change its rule about no students inside until the first bell—at least during the winter months. They might all freeze to death while they waited! But she supposed it kept kids from arriving on the campus too early. She would gladly put off her arrival, but she had to ride the bus, and the driver always dropped her off first.

Shivering, she leaned against the cold window and looked across the grounds at the other students, who huddled in little circles, blowing on their hands and shifting from foot to foot. She spotted Paul and Marlys, and she couldn't resist giving a little wave with her mitten-covered hand. Paul waved back, but Marlys just pulled her scarf snugly around her neck as if she hadn't seen Katy wave.

Katy sighed, her breath hanging in the air. She supposed she didn't have to be friends with Marlys, but it would be nice if the girl would at least be a little friendly. After all, they were debate squad partners. And their names would be together on that trophy.

"Katy!"

Katy spun around when she heard Shelby's cheerful voice. Shelby and Jewel scurried toward her across the dried grass. Shelby's face wore its customary smile and Jewel's the far-too-familiar scowl. Those two girls were as different as night and day. Katy wondered how they managed to live under the same roof.

Shelby plopped her backpack on the cement by her feet then flashed Katy a wide grin. "How did the debate tournament go? I wanted to call you yesterday to find out."

For the hundredth time, Katy wished she and Dad had a telephone in their house. But they had to use the one at the restaurant in Schellberg, like the other fellowship members. Telephones were an intrusion, her fellowship believed, but Dad thought maybe the church would lift the ban against them someday. Katy hoped it was soon.

Her chest puffed with pride when she answered. "We got third place."

Shelby squealed. "Sweet!" She punched Jewel's shoulder. "See? I told you Katy would rock 'em."

Jewel grunted, shifting away from Shelby. "Yeah, you told me. Way to go, Katy." Although Jewel's tone lacked enthusiasm, Katy decided not to be insulted. Jewel always acted bored, and Katy had learned the girl used her tone as a mask for her real feelings.

"Thanks. We got a trophy and everything, and Mr. Gorsky said our names will be imprinted on it. Then it'll go in the trophy case." Katy peeked through the window at the long, glass-enclosed cases that lined the walls of the foyer. For the rest of the school's existence, the trophy she helped win would be in that case as a reminder that she'd been here. She smiled, thinking about it.

"So will you be going to any more tournaments before Christmas break?" Shelby bounced on her heels, hugging herself. Her breath came out in little puffs.

Disappointment sagged Katy's shoulders. "No. That was the last novice tournament, and Mr. Gorsky has enough experienced debaters to fill the remaining tournaments. That was my only chance this year." Then she brightened. "But I plan to debate next year too, if Dad lets me stay in school."

Jewel snorted. "I wish I had the choice to stay in school or not. I have to stay in as long as the state has control of me. But if I was living with my mom, she'd probably let me get my GED instead."

Katy sent Shelby a quick look. Jewel was in a really sour mood this morning. Shelby raised one eyebrow and nodded, as if agreeing with Katy's secret thoughts. The bell rang, and Jewel shot through the doors. Shelby looped elbows with Katy and followed more slowly.

"Jewel was supposed to spend the weekend with her mom, but her mom cancelled." Shelby kept her voice low so the kids crowding around them wouldn't hear. "She's really bummed. She wants out of foster care pretty badly, but until her mom meets the requirement and makes her boyfriend move out of the house ..."

Katy had seen Jewel's house, her mom's boyfriend, and the way her mother lived. If she were Jewel, she'd rather stay with Shelby's family as a foster child in their clean, happy home than go back to the awful place Jewel's mother called home. Yet she couldn't blame Jewel for wanting to be with her mother. If Katy's mother were still alive, she would be tempted to live with her, no matter where that might be.

Midway through the first-hour class, the PA system suddenly clicked on and the principal's voice interrupted the biology teacher's lecture on the separation of cells.

"Ladies and gentlemen, I have an announcement. This past weekend at the Dodge City Novice Invitational Debate Tournament—"

A pleasant chill skittered up Katy's spine. She nearly giggled.

"—our debate team made up of members Paul Andress, Marlys Horton, Kathleen Lambright, and Bryce Porter took third place. Congratulations to these students and their coach, Mr. Gorsky. Let's give them a round of applause."

Half-hearted applause pattered across the biology room. One of the boys hooted, "Go, Kathleen!" Several students snickered at his outburst, but Shelby patted Katy on the back and whistled loudly. Katy sent a shy smile around the room. Were Bryce, Marlys, and Paul receiving heartier congratulations in their classrooms right now?

Then the principal's voice came on again, ending the cheers. "Thank you, Mr. Gorsky, Paul, Marlys, Kathleen, and Bryce, for representing our school so well. We wish success to all of our debaters in the final tournaments of the season." The PA system clicked off.

The teacher walked over and shook Katy's hand. "Congratulations, Kathleen." He immediately returned to his lecture, as if the interruption hadn't occurred, but Katy had a hard time concentrating. Success—even when few people celebrated enthusiastically—was exhilarating. Hearing her name announced over the intercom had been embarrassing but thrilling. Even though she'd been taught from the time she was a little girl that she shouldn't be prideful, she couldn't swallow the feelings of satisfaction. She was a good debater. The trophy proved it.

When Katy entered Mr. Gorsky's class for English, he quirked his finger at her to come to his desk. Her face hot, she dropped her backpack next to her chair and scurried to the front of the room. He pointed at a paper on his desk.

"I'll be taking the trophy in for engraving after debate practice this afternoon. I just want you to double-check the spelling on your name to be sure it's correct."

Katy looked at the paper, where her name — KATHLEEN LAMBRIGHT — was printed in neat block letters. She nodded. "It's perfect."

Mr. Gorsky held out a pen. "Good. Put a check mark next to it."

Katy followed his instruction. "When do you think the trophy will be done?"

"Probably within a week — before Christmas break, certainly."

Katy handed back his pen. Tangling her hands in the fabric of her skirt, she said, "Will I be scorekeeping for everybody at practice after school today, since I won't be debating again?"

A thoughtful frown creased Mr. Gorsky's brow. "Hmm, I hadn't thought about that. Actually, Kathleen, since there are just three weeks left in the season, if you'd rather take the early bus after school, you probably wouldn't need to come to practice anymore."

"I — I don't need to come?"

Mr. Gorsky didn't seem to notice the tremble in her voice. "It really isn't necessary since you won't be able to debate again until next year." He smiled, unaware of how much his words hurt. "But it's up to you. You're certainly welcome to come in and do the scorekeeping, if you'd like."

"Th-thank you." Katy scuffed her way to her desk and sat down, defeated. She'd helped win a trophy, but now she wasn't needed. All of the warm feelings that had carried her through the morning slipped away.

The class opened their copies of Oscar Wilde's *The Importance of Being Earnest* and began discussing the author's viewpoint that style was more vital than sincerity. Although Katy normally joined eagerly into class discussions, today she stayed silent. When class ended, Katy hurried out the door ahead of everyone else. Shelby caught up to her and grabbed her arm.

"Katy, are you okay?"

The genuine concern in Shelby's voice made tears sting behind Katy's nose. She sniffed. "I'm fine."

"The way the kids acted in biology didn't bother you, did it? They never get very excited about debate or music stuff. They save their cheers for the football or basketball teams. Don't take it personally."

Kay hurried on. "I'm not."

"I've never seen you so quiet." Shelby tugged Katy over to the wall and stopped, allowing the other students to go on past them. "Are you sure somebody didn't say something stupid to you? Like maybe Jewel?"

There had been times in the past when Jewel had hurt Katy's feelings, but Katy couldn't blame Jewel for her change in mood. Not this time. "Jewel didn't do anything. I'm just a ... a little bummed"—she borrowed one of Shelby's words—"because the debate season is over. I really liked getting to debate in that tournament." She swallowed hard when tears threatened.

"Aw, I'm sorry, Katy." Shelby squeezed Katy's arm. "But there's always next year, you know. And forensics next semester. So you'll still get to compete. It won't be your only tournament."

"I guess so ..."

At that moment Bryce bustled by, and Shelby called, "Bryce! Come here a minute."

Bryce spun around and leaned against the wall next Shelby. "Hey, what's up?"

"You were part of forensics last year, weren't you?"

Bryce nodded. "Yep, why?" He sent a grin toward Katy that made her heart skip a beat.

Shelby said, "Katy really likes to debate, so what can you do in forensics that's close to debating?"

Bryce scratched his head. "Well, there are a couple of things, actually. You can do extemporaneous speaking, where you draw a topic from a hat and have thirty minutes to prepare a seven-minute talk on the topic."

Katy licked her lips. That sounded pretty hard.

"Or there's original oration. You choose a topic you really care about and write a seven-minute speech that's meant to convince the judge that your point of view is the right one." Bryce shrugged. "The only difference is nobody's arguing with you on the spot—it's just you giving your opinion."

Katy felt her lips twitching into a smile. "I think I could do that."

"Yeah, you're a good writer and a good speaker. Original oration would be perfect for you."

Katy's knees started to quake. Bryce thought she was a good writer and speaker! Her ears burned with happiness.

Bryce took two backward steps, bouncing his grin from one girl to the other. "Lunch is calling. See you after school, Katy." He whirled and trotted around the corner.

"So, see?" Shelby offered an encouraging smile. "You'll still get to use those debating skills. Now, c'mon, let's get to the cafeteria before the lunch period is over."

Katy deposited her backpack in her locker and walked with Shelby to the cafeteria. She replayed Shelby's comment about using her debating skills, and she fought a giggle. Of course she'd be using her debating skills — with Dad.

By the time lunch was over, she'd decided not to go to any more debate practices. Mr. Gorsky had said it wasn't necessary, and she trusted his opinion. Plus if she went home right after school, she'd have more time with Dad to show him how well she could meet all of the challenges of schoolwork, helping in the dairy, caring for the house, and staying out of trouble without anyone else's assistance.

At the next table, Bryce suddenly burst out laughing. Katy turned around, and he caught her eye. He grinned and winked before looking away, and warmth flooded Katy's ears and her face. She bent over her tray and focused on the chicken and noodles. Even though going home was the best idea, she kind of wished she didn't have to. She'd miss that time with Bryce every day.

Chapter Eight

Katy slipped her sweater over her dress and dashed across the yard toward the barn. Caleb Penner's sedan blocked the path, forcing her to take a detour. But she wouldn't complain! The chilly wind chased her through the big door. She scurried into the tank room, where milk flowed through clear tubes into the large refrigerated tank. When Katy was little, she liked to pretend the tank was a hippopotamus. Sometimes she wished she were still little. Life had been a lot less complicated back then.

She tapped on the thick glass window that offered a view into the milking room. Both Dad and Caleb lifted their heads from the milking machines. Even the cows hooked to the machines looked up. Katy grinned at the curious bovine faces then focused on Dad. She mimed lifting a spoon to her mouth then pointed to the back of her left wrist to ask when he would be ready to eat. Usually he and Caleb were finished milking by 6:30, but it was already 6:45, and a few cows still waited in line outside the barn.

Dad balled his fists and flashed his fingers twice, telling Katy he needed twenty more minutes. She tried not to frown. Her meatloaf would be dry and flavorless by then. Before she could acknowledge his response, he pointed at Caleb and held up three fingers. Katy got the message: set three plates because Caleb was staying for supper. Another frown tried to curl her lips downward, but she managed to hold it at bay and scurried out of the barn back to the kitchen.

The good smells from the oven turned her stomach inside-out with hunger when she entered the house. She wished she could go ahead and eat. The meatloaf, fried potatoes, and canned peas were ready. And if she ate now, she wouldn't have to sit at the table with Caleb, listening to him smack his food. Why hadn't Mrs. Penner taught him better manners? But Dad wouldn't approve of her eating ahead of him and their guest, so she pushed her hunger aside and removed another plate from the cabinet.

As she plunked the plate and silverware on the table, she muttered, "At least I'm not setting a plate for Mrs. Graber." A second thought immediately followed. With Caleb as their guest this evening, she had the chance to show Dad she could be a gracious hostess, something most girls learned from their mothers. *Dad will see I already have the skills needed to host guests at our table—one less reason to need Mrs. Graber.*

Humming, Katy scuttled to the glass-front china hutch her mother had left behind and retrieved their best napkins, ones Gramma Ruthie had embroidered for Katy's parents as a wedding gift. She folded them into neat triangles and arranged the silverware in precise rows on the creamy linen. Then she scrounged in the highest cabinet for a pretty bowl. She couldn't put a vase of flowers in the middle of the table, but the bowl filled with red and green apples from the refrigerator would make a nice splash of color against the plain brown wood of the table. She arranged the apples just so, balancing the two colors perfectly against each other.

Instead of leaving the food in the cooking pans, the way she always did when it was just her and Dad at the table, she transferred the meatloaf to a plate and scooped the potatoes and peas into serving bowls. She even put ketchup for the meatloaf and potatoes in a little bowl with a spoon instead of plopping the plastic bottle on the table.

She had just finished filling the glasses with milk when the back door opened and Dad and Caleb pounded into the room. They carried the smell of the barn with them, and Katy almost wrinkled her nose. But she caught herself in time, whisked off her apron, and invited, "Wash up at the sink, then we can eat. Everything's hot and ready to go."

She waited until Dad and Caleb sat before sliding into her seat. Dad said grace, then she offered him the platter of sliced meatloaf. She turned to Caleb. "Help yourself to the potatoes, Caleb."

Caleb snatched up the bowl and dumped half of its contents onto his plate. Instead of handing her the bowl, which would have been the polite thing for him to do, he put it back on the table and looked around, his forehead scrunched into a frown. "Do you have any bread? I like to sop up the grease from fried potatoes with bread."

Katy nearly shuddered in revulsion. But she forced a smile. "Why, certainly." She skipped to the breadbox and pulled out the plastic bag of bread. She stacked several

71

slices on a dessert plate and carried it to the table. "Would you like butter too?"

Caleb gawked at the plate. "Store-bought bread?"

Store-bought won't absorb grease? Katy nearly bit her tongue in two, holding the sarcastic comment inside. "Yes, Dad bought a loaf at the store."

"Ma always bakes our bread." Caleb stared at the bread like he expected it to jump off the plate and attack him.

She tightened her fingers on the plate to keep from bopping him over the head with it. "I'm sorry, but I wasn't home this past Saturday to bake." Amazing how sweet she sounded considering her extreme aggravation. *Good job, Katy. Smile. Be pleasant. Dad's listening.* "Do you still want some, even though it's store-bought?"

Dad cleared his throat. "I'll take some. And some butter. Thanks, Katy-girl."

Katy gave Dad the bread and retrieved the butter dish from the refrigerator. She sat back down and carefully smoothed her napkin over her lap. Caleb had tucked his napkin into his shirt collar. *No manners whatsoever ...* She filled her plate with the now cold meatloaf, potatoes, and peas. She also took a piece of bread, slathered it with butter, and smiled as she bit into it. She would eat every bit of the bread even if it was as flavorless as a tissue.

"Milk production's down about five percent," Dad commented. He took another bite of meatloaf, chewed, and swallowed. "'Course, I expect that to happen when the weather cools down."

"Less milk means less money." Caleb spoke around a huge bite of potatoes.

Katy almost rolled her eyes. Any idiot could reach that

conclusion. She glanced at Caleb. A blob of ketchup decorated the corner of his mouth. She quickly looked at Dad. "We'll be fine. We always have been."

"My dad gets less business during the winter months too." Caleb's words slurred around the peas in his mouth. He shoveled in another scoop. "But he's smart. He puts aside extra money during the summer so he won't have to worry when things slow down."

Katy bristled. Was Caleb insinuating that Dad was too stupid to take care of his own finances? She gritted her teeth before she said something she'd regret.

"Oh, I think most of us around here know to do that." Dad replied in a calm tone. "But I do need to let you know I plan on having Katy help me during her Christmas break from school, so you'll get a little break too."

Caleb licked his lips, removing most of the ketchup. "You sure? I don't mind coming over."

"I know, and I appreciate it," Dad said. He winked at Katy. "But she won't have homework during the break, so she can help me."

Katy battled conflicting emotions — elation that she'd get a break from Caleb coming to her house every day and disappointment that she'd be stuck out in the dairy barn twice a day during her break. She had hoped to spend that extra time catching up on her journal writing and maybe sewing a new dress or two. But she smiled. "That sounds fine, Dad. I'll be glad to help you."

Caleb shot her a doubtful look. "Well, Mr. Lambright, I guess you know what you're doing, but a girl ..."

Had Caleb forgotten that *a girl* was Dad's only help before Dad hired him? The cows hadn't seemed to mind being hooked up to the machine by *a girl*. She snorted, then covered the sound by coughing lightly into her napkin. She turned her sweetest smile on Caleb. "Thank you for your concern, but you don't need to worry. I'm stronger than I look, and I'm very familiar with milking." *Duh. I've only grown up on this dairy farm, you freckle-faced doofus. You're the newcomer around here.* "You just enjoy that break with your family."

Caleb sighed. "Oh, I'll enjoy the break, but I'll miss the paycheck. Can I have more of that meatloaf?"

"*May* I have —" Katy started to correct Caleb, but then she realized what she was doing. With a quick glance at Dad, she finished, "The honor of serving you?" She stabbed a slice of meatloaf and held it toward Caleb's plate. He picked up his plate and let Katy place the meatloaf next to his remaining potatoes. "Would you like some ketchup?"

"Yeah." Caleb spooned several dollops of the red paste onto the meat. "It needs it. It's good but kind of dry."

Katy swallowed a yelp. Dad covered his mouth with his napkin. His shoulders shook slightly. She looked at Dad closely. Was he *laughing*? She didn't know what aggravated her more — Caleb's bad-mannered behavior or Dad's amusement.

Drawing in a deep breath, she lifted her chin. "It had to stay in the oven a little longer than usual since dinner was late tonight. I'm sorry."

Caleb shrugged and forked up a big bite. "Oh, don't worry about it, Katydid. If you put in more onions next time, it'll keep it from drying out. That's what my mom does. Her meatloaf is tops."

Soft grunts came from behind Dad's napkin, and Katy knew he was laughing. If only she hadn't decided to be the gracious hostess, she'd let both men have an earful! But all she could do was smile.

Dad dropped his napkin back into his lap and continued eating. A funny grin twitched on the corners of his lips, but he didn't do any more laughing. When he'd emptied his plate, he said, "Did you make dessert, Katy?"

There was ice cream in the freezer, but Katy decided she didn't want to prolong dinner if she could avoid it. The sooner Caleb left, the better. She might not be able to hold her tongue much longer. "Not tonight. Sorry."

"That's all right." Dad plucked a green apple from the bowl in the middle of the table. The others tumbled together, ruining the perfect balance of colors she'd created. "Get me a paring knife, and I'll just slice up an apple for dessert."

"Me too." Caleb grabbed out a red one.

Katy fetched two paring knives, nearly groaning in frustration. Why hadn't she just served the ice cream? It would take less time to eat a bowl of ice cream than it would to peel, slice, and eat an apple. By the time Caleb finished and used the napkin to clean the remaining ketchup from his mouth, Katy was ready to collapse from the strain of being pleasant. But she still managed to walk him to the door, wait while he zipped up his coat, then hold the screen door open for him.

"Good-bye, Caleb. Enjoy the rest of your evening now."

"Yeah, I will." He started out the door, but then he turned back. "Oh, Katydid?"

"Yes?" Would he finally thank her for the meal? It might erase some of her irritation with him.

"This coming Saturday, the Brauns are planning a singing and popcorn-stringing party over at their place. Do you wanna go with me?" Caleb's face glowed so red his freckles almost disappeared.

Katy stared at him in amazement. After he'd suggested she wasn't capable of seeing to the cows, insulted her cooking, then failed to offer a polite thank-you for feeding him, he had the nerve to invite her to a party?

Dad's chair legs scraped against the wood floor. He crossed behind Katy and put his hand on her shoulder. "We'll talk about it and let you know tomorrow, Caleb. Good-night now."

"Oh, okay. Sure. Tomorrow then." Caleb scuttled out the door.

Dad stepped around Katy and closed the door behind Caleb. Then he faced Katy. He chuckled. "So do you want to go to the popcorn-stringing party with Caleb?"

Katy folded her arms over her chest and let her expression provide the answer.

Dad's chuckle rumbled again. "That's what I thought. Okay, I'll tell him tomorrow that it isn't going to work for you to go with him."

Katy sighed. "Thanks, Dad."

Dad reached out and tugged Katy into a hug. "I know he bothers you, but he's young yet. When he finally grows up, he won't be so annoying."

She didn't know if she believed that Caleb would ever become less annoying, but it felt good to have Dad understand her feelings. Katy burrowed into his chest, wrapping her arms tightly around his waist.

He patted her back and released her. He frowned at the

table. "I guess you've got a mess to clean up now, huh? Do you want some help?"

Oh, to have help with all those dishes! But she couldn't accept it — then she'd seem incapable of handling it alone. She shook her head so hard her ribbons flew. "No, I'm fine. You go read the paper or something."

"All right then." He smiled down at her. "I was proud of you tonight. Thank you for being so courteous even though it was hard for you." He ambled toward the living room.

Katy watched him go, her ears ringing with his praise. *Dad 1 – Katy 2.* Those were the words she wanted to hear. She should have celebrated that her plan worked to show Dad how grown-up and mature she could be. But instead, tears stung. Why did she feel guilty instead of happy?

Chapter Nine

Katy settled at the desk in her room. She needed to do homework—instead, she reached for her journal. She thought back on the evening with Caleb at the table, and in spite of her earlier irritation, she giggled. Almost without effort, she formed a poem on the page.

Ode to an Unpleasant Night
He was sitting at the table,
But it might have been a stable
The way he gnawed and smacked and chomped his food.
With freckles his nose dotting
And ketchup his mouth blotting,
Oblivious, he ruined his hostess's mood.
He dared to offer insult
With an unexpected result—
Her father recognized how rudely crude
Was this dinner guest's behavior.
And then to her great favor
Right out the door the bumbling pest was shooed.

She covered her mouth to hold back her laughter. If Dad

heard her up here laughing, he might investigate, and she didn't plan to share this poem with anyone. Except maybe Shelby. Shelby would see the humor in it. She drew little curlicues around the edges, decorating the poem, but as the pencil traced whirls on the page, she remembered her strange reaction to Dad's compliment.

She stilled her pencil. She bit down on her lower lip, odd emotions nibbling at the edges of her mind. Turning to a clean page, she haltingly wrote a different poem.

> *So many feelings inside of me.*
> *I don't know … who should I be:*
> *A girl who pleases everyone else*
> *Or one who only serves herself?*
> *My conscience bids me do what's right,*
> *But frankness begs to be given flight.*
> *Inside I long to rant and rage*
> *Against the rules that form my cage.*
> *But if I break from these restraints,*
> *Will I find freedom … or merely pain?*

She stared at the words, seeking answers to the questions the poem raised. Showing herself competent and too grown-up to require a mother's care remained her goal. Dad's reaction to her performance as the perfect hostess this evening proved she could do it. But Annika had said pretending was the same as lying, and Katy didn't want to be a liar. No one trusted a liar. Besides that, the Bible told stories about God's judgment falling on those who practiced dishonesty.

Katy wondered: *Was keeping Dad from marrying Mrs. Graber worth risking God's wrath?*

Wednesday morning, before the opening school bell, Katy joined the student Bible study group in the home economics classroom. The group had gained several new members since the weather had turned cooler, and Katy suspected a few of the people were only there to avoid standing outside. When she said as much to Shelby, Shelby laughed and replied, "Well, if they're here listening, maybe they'll pick up on something good. You never know!" Katy hoped Shelby was right.

Today's reading came from Second Corinthians, chapter five, and verse seventeen in particular pierced Katy's spirit. "Therefore, if anyone is in Christ, he is a new creation — the old has gone, the new has come!" Katy knew she was a new creation in Christ — she had accepted His gift of salvation when she was eleven years old. But she still struggled against the old, selfish spirit. Why did it have to be so hard to be a new creature?

At the end of the study time, the leader asked Bryce to close the meeting. Katy lowered her head and listened as Bryce stammered out a quick prayer. Katy wondered why someone who was so eloquent in a debate round had so much trouble expressing a simple prayer. But speaking was different than praying. She'd never prayed aloud in a room full of people — the men in her church fellowship always offered the public prayers. She might stammer too.

"Amen," Bryce said, and everyone gathered their backpacks to leave. Katy flung her flowered backpack over one shoulder, the way the other kids carried theirs, and headed for the door.

Bryce sidled up next to her. "You weren't at debate practice last night. How come?"

"Mr. Gorsky said I won't be able to participate in any other meets, so it was okay if I just went on home."

"That makes sense." Bryce shifted the weight of his backpack, bumping her lightly with his shoulder. "But it's too bad." He grinned. "I got kind of used to seeing you in debate. I missed you."

Katy thought her heart might fly right out of her chest. "Really?"

"Really. You're the only girl in debate a guy can talk to without feeling like an idiot."

A lot of the time, Katy was uncomfortable around the other debate kids. They kept their distance from her, probably because of her Mennonite dress and cap. But Bryce wasn't Mennonite. Why would *he* feel like an idiot talking to Marlys, Vicki, or any of the other girls? She wanted to ask, but her tongue felt stuck to the roof of her mouth, and she couldn't form the question.

They reached the lockers, and Bryce lifted his hand in a wave. "Oh, well. I'll still see you around, right? And you'll be participating in forensics?"

Katy nodded. She'd definitely be in forensics.

"Okay then. Have a good day, Katy." He jogged to his locker and began talking to a couple of other kids.

Katy stood staring after him. Bryce and Caleb looked a lot alike. They both had red hair, although Caleb's was more red than blond and Bryce's more blond than red; they were nearly the same height and build; and both had a spattering of freckles. But while Caleb made Katy want to run the opposite direction, she had no desire to run away from Bryce. She liked Bryce. He wasn't Mennonite, but he was nice. She wished he'd have talked to her a little longer.

Someone tapped her arm, and reluctantly she shifted her attention away from Bryce. Shelby stood grinning at her. "Did you look in the trophy case when you got to school this morning?"

Katy shook her head. She'd been in a hurry to get to the home ec room before the Bible study began. Her pulse sped up. "Is it there?"

"It's there." Shelby tugged her down the hall. "C'mon. The warning bell will ring in a few minutes, but we've got time for a peek."

The girls trotted to the front foyer, and Shelby led Katy to the case holding debate trophies. Right in front, on a low shelf, sat the trophy she helped win. She pressed her nose to the glass and let out a giggle. "Oh, look! There's my name." *Right next to Bryce's.* She liked the way their names looked together.

"Yep. Totally cool." Shelby rested her shoulder against the glass and shook her head. "It would scare me to death to get up in front of judges and argue like you did. But your first time out, you get a trophy. It's gotta feel good."

"Well ..." Katy ducked her head, pushing down the feeling of pride that tried to rise. "I didn't get it all on my own. Paul, Marlys, and Bryce helped."

"I suppose that's true. But, still, you had to do your part or you guys wouldn't have won." Shelby made a face. "My dad wants me to do debate at least one year. He says it helps prepare you for the future."

Katy tore her gaze away from the trophy to look at Shelby. "Really? How?"

"He says no matter what job a person gets, there are always times you have to present yourself to others. You have to be confident enough to speak your mind. So he's encouraging me to do debate next year."

Katy couldn't help but smile. "That would be great, Shelby. If the deacons and my dad let me come back next year, then maybe we could be partners." *Unless I can be partners with Bryce* ... Would she really choose Bryce over Shelby?

"If I could be your partner, it might be okay." Shelby didn't look certain. "I don't know for sure if I'll do it. I'm still thinking about it."

"But your dad really thinks it's a good thing to learn to ... to speak your mind?"

"Well, sure. Otherwise people run right over the top of you." Shelby pushed her streaky blonde hair behind her ears. "I mean, we're Christians, so we aren't supposed to be mean and pushy about it, but if we never speak up, how will people know what we believe? Dad preaches a lot about speaking the truth in love. It takes courage to do that."

Thoughts bounced around in Katy's brain. She grabbed Shelby's wrist. "Shelby, do you think it's ever okay to do something, well, sort of sneaky, if the reason for it is good?"

Shelby frowned. "Sneaky? Like a surprise or something?"

"Not a surprise really. Just to keep something bad from happening."

Shelby shrugged. "I don't know how stopping something bad from happening could be wrong. I mean, take Jewel. She wants to go back to her mom really badly. But the social worker and my folks know it wouldn't be best for her, so they keep her living with us. She doesn't always like it, but it's really for her good."

Katy nodded eagerly. "So doing something that's for someone's good, even if they might not see it that way, really is right."

"I guess so." Shelby grinned. "What're you doing anyway? You don't have a foster kid living with you."

And if she had her way, Katy wouldn't have a stepmother living with her either. "Oh, nothing really. I just wondered what you thought." She hadn't been completely truthful. Her conscience pricked again. She could tell Shelby about her plan to keep Dad from marrying Mrs. Graber. Shelby wasn't as critical as Annika. She'd surely understand.

Katy opened her mouth, but Shelby said, "Oh, before I forget, would you pray for Bridget's family? Her dad lost his job, and he needs another one fast or they'll lose their house. Bridget is pretty worried about it."

Katy nodded. "Of course I will. And can I talk to you about something?"

"Sure," Shelby said, but the buzzer rang, signaling the start of first hour. "But later, huh? We better get to class." Shelby headed for the hallway, and Katy walked alongside her. The opportunity to share slipped away, and by the end of first hour Katy decided that was okay. The fewer people who knew her plan, the better.

Chapter Ten

The final week of first semester flew by, and Katy could hardly believe Christmas was just around the corner. Although the weather had been cold, they still hadn't gotten any snow. Katy felt a little selfish, but she prayed for snow for Christmas. Somehow it just didn't feel right to celebrate that special holiday unless the ground held a covering of white.

The first Saturday of her break, Dad woke her at five o'clock in the morning to go out to the barn and help with the milking. Katy hadn't fully appreciated Caleb's presence, but she begrudgingly changed her mind as she tugged on coveralls, stumbled into the milking room, and set to work. Her fingers were clumsy after her long break from helping with the milking. Dad didn't get after her, even though his cows shuffled through much more quickly than the ones on her side of the room.

She yawned while she worked and wished she could go back up to bed, but after they finished milking she'd need to fix breakfast then get ready for her and Dad's trip to the Salina mall. When they got home again, she had housecleaning to do. But at least no homework! Two whole weeks without homework. That gave her a reason to smile.

When the last cow ambled out to the pasture, Dad shut off the machines and grinned at Katy. "I'll feed them while you're cooking breakfast. Waffles sound good to me."

Katy's stomach growled. She scrambled out of her coveralls and reached up to put them on their hook. "To me too." And waffles were easy—that made it even better.

"Then after we eat, we can relax a little bit before we head for Salina. The mall doesn't open until nine o'clock, so we don't need to be in a big rush."

Katy yawned again. "So maybe I can take a nap before we leave?"

Dad laughed. "A short one maybe. But hurry on into the house now and get those waffles started. I'm hungry."

Two hours later, Dad and Katy climbed into Dad's pickup and set off down the road. Katy searched the sky for signs of snow. The sky was the same color as the old galvanized tub that sat beside the back steps and held the flowers Katy planted in the summertime. Solid gray. She sighed and looked at Dad. "Do you think we'll have snow for Christmas?"

Dad glanced at the sky too, then shrugged. "Hard to say, Katy-girl. You know how quickly the weather changes around here. I know the farmers are hoping for snow— ground needs the moisture."

"I'm praying for snow," she said, and Dad sent an approving smile in her direction. She knew he thought her prayers were for the farmers rather than herself, but she didn't correct him. She liked seeing him smile.

He slowed the truck and turned onto the road that led

to Schellberg instead of driving straight to the highway. Katy frowned. "Aren't we going to the mall?"

"Sure we are."

"But the mall's that way." She pointed east.

"I know, but we need to trade vehicles at Grampa's place and pick up Mrs. Graber."

Katy's mouth fell open. "Mrs. Graber is coming too?"

"Didn't I tell you that?"

"No. You just said *we'd* be going."

Dad scratched his chin. "I thought I did. It must have slipped my mind. I'm sorry, Katy-girl." He sounded sincere. "She wants to do some last-minute shopping too, and she isn't as familiar with Salina as we are. So she asked to go along. Is that all right with you?"

Katy had looked forward to a day with Dad. But how could she gracefully refuse? And hadn't she been hoping for the chance to be extra nice to the woman so Dad could see she didn't need a mother's influence? She tossed her cap ribbons over her shoulders. "Sure it's all right. She hasn't come out as much since the weather turned cold. It'll be nice to see her."

Dad's eyebrows shot up like Katy had surprised him, but then he smiled. "Well, good!" Dad reached across the seat and squeezed Katy's shoulder. Even through her coat, she felt the warmth of his hand. "I know she's looking forward to some time with us too."

A funny feeling wiggled through Katy's stomach. This pretending wasn't easy. "Then let's go."

The minute Katy and Dad hopped out of the truck, Mrs. Graber stepped onto the porch. She wore a dark green wool coat that made her eyes look as green as clover. She smiled and waved. "You're right on time, Samuel!" Her smile shifted to Katy. "Hello, Kathleen. I imagine you're happy to be on break."

Apparently, Dad discussed Katy's schedule with Mrs. Graber. Katy felt her lips quiver with her smile. "Yes. It's nice to have some time off. But I'll be ready to go back too."

"Oh, yes, you're an eager learner. That's a good thing."

How weird that this woman knew so much about her. Katy didn't know what to say, so she hunched deeper into her coat and turned to Dad. "Whose car are we taking? Grampa Ben's?"

"No, we're taking mine," Mrs. Graber answered. She dropped a ring of keys into Dad's hand. "But your dad is going to drive us. I don't care to drive in unfamiliar cities."

Katy followed Dad and Mrs. Graber to her four-door sedan. She couldn't resist diving on the opening Mrs. Graber had provided. "I bet you'll be really happy to be back in Meschke then, where you know all the streets and feel completely at ease."

"I am very at home in Meschke," Mrs. Graber replied, seemingly unoffended by Katy's comment. "But since Schellberg isn't any bigger, I don't feel ill-at-ease here, either." She laughed lightly. "Salina, however, is different!"

Dad opened the front passenger door and gestured for Mrs. Graber to get in. He slammed the door and then glanced at Katy. "Hop in, Katy-girl—it's cold out here."

He didn't seem perturbed. Apparently, her tone had met with his approval. But he hadn't opened her door, the way he did for Mrs. Graber. Stifling a growl, Katy climbed in behind Mrs. Graber. Dad slid behind the wheel, adjusted the seat and the mirrors, and started the motor. He shot a quick look at Katy. "Buckle up, Katy-girl." As soon as she snapped in, he pulled out of the yard and aimed the car for the highway.

He looked awfully comfortable driving Mrs. Graber's car. Katy wondered if he'd driven it some other time already. The two grown-ups chatted, apparently forgetting Katy sat in the backseat. She folded her arms over her chest and glared at the little white cap on Mrs. Graber's head. Her excitement for the shopping venture faded fast as Mrs. Graber and Dad laughed and talked like old friends. Why had she even bothered to come if they weren't going to include her?

Don't pout, she reminded herself. *Be nice. Remember your plan.*

Katy waited for a break in the conversation then tapped Mrs. Graber on the shoulder. "Mrs. Graber, who are you shopping for today?"

Mrs. Graber shifted slightly to smile into the backseat. "I have almost all of my gift-buying done, but I need some fabric to sew kitchen curtains for my daughter. She and her husband just moved into a bigger house, and she doesn't like the curtains in the kitchen. So I said I'd make some for her."

Katy knew very little about Mrs. Graber's family. Gramma Ruthie had mentioned Mrs. Graber had three children, all grown, but that's all Katy knew. "Does she live in Meschke?"

Mrs. Graber shook her head. For a moment, sadness sagged her face. "No. She moved to Iowa when she got married two years ago." Then she smiled. "But my oldest son lives in Meschke, on our family farm, and my younger son is nearby in Meade. We'll all be together for Christmas too."

"So you're going to Meschke for Christmas?" Katy asked. She hoped she didn't sound too eager to get rid of the woman.

"Yes, I'm looking forward to it."

Dad inserted, "But she'll be back in mid-January." He glanced at her. "Right?"

Mrs. Graber turned to smile at Dad's profile. "Yes. I promised the fellowship ladies I'd help finish that quilt for the relief sale."

"And after that?" Katy knew she probably shouldn't ask, but she couldn't stop herself.

Mrs. Graber kept her face aimed at Dad. "After that . . . we'll see."

Katy quickly looked out the window. The "we'll see" sounded like a hint to Dad. Her thoughts raced. If Mrs. Graber left before Christmas and didn't come back until mid-January, she'd have three weeks to show Dad how unnecessary the woman was. Her skin tingled in anticipation. She could do a lot of convincing in three weeks.

Dad turned into the mall parking lot. The lot was crowded, and he had to park at the far end away from the main entrance. The wind stung Katy's cheeks as she trotted toward the mall. She walked as close to Dad's side as possible, allowing his larger bulk to block some of the wind. Mrs. Graber walked on his other side, close enough that her elbow and Dad's pressed against each other. Katy tried not to stare.

Inside, Dad shrugged out of his coat and draped it over his arm. "So where to first?" Instead of looking at Katy, he looked at Mrs. Graber.

Katy unbuttoned her coat and purposely bumped Dad's

arm with her elbow. "Can we go to the craft store first? I want to look for some of those plaques decorated with inspirational sayings or Bible verses."

Dad tucked his arm closer to his side. "Is that all right with you, Rosemary?"

Since when had this shopping day become Mrs. Graber's day? Irritation prickled through Katy's middle, and she bit the end of her tongue to keep from complaining.

"Just fine. I enjoy browsing craft stores."

Dad took hold of Mrs. Graber's elbow and guided her down the tiled walkway toward the craft store. Katy tried to walk alongside him, but other shoppers bustling through the wide hall forced her to drop behind. When they reached the craft store, Dad paused and gestured Katy to catch up.

"I'm not sure which section you need. Lead the way."

Temptation to loop her arm through Dad's elbow and keep him close billowed like a storm cloud. For as long as she could remember, she'd taken second place to the cows. Now she was being forced to take third place — behind the cows *and* Mrs. Graber. Katy wanted to grit her teeth and tell Dad how unfair he was being — instead, she flashed a quick grin and darted around the two adults. "Come with me." The display of wooden and tin plaques was pretty picked over, but Katy found two she liked. She held both at arm's length, trying to decide.

"What do you think, Dad? Which one would Annika like best?"

Dad shook his head and held up his hands. "I wouldn't know, Katy."

Mrs. Graber stepped forward and carefully examined

both plaques. "Isn't Annika the girl whose sister in getting married in January?"

Katy nodded. "Yes. Taryn is marrying her beau."

"Well, then, she's probably feeling a little left out with all the attention on her sister. So I think the one that says *You are loved*."

Katy liked that one best too. The flowing script reminded her of the fancy calligraphy Annika liked to do, and the saying could mean Annika was loved by God, her family, and Katy. But even so, for one brief second, Katy considered putting it back just because Mrs. Graber had selected it. Quickly, before she could change her mind, she put the other one on the shelf.

"Okay. That's for Annika. All I have left is Gramma Ruthie."

Dad began walking toward the row of checkout counters at the front of the store. Katy fell into step behind Dad, and Mrs. Graber stayed beside her. Between dodging shopping carts and other shoppers, they made slow progress. Mrs. Graber asked, "What did you have in mind for your grandma?"

The past two years, she'd made aprons for Gramma Ruthie. She didn't want to do that again. "Maybe some placemats and matching napkins ..." Katy mused aloud. "She has people over for meals so often, I thought she might like some new ones."

"That's a fine idea, Kathleen. So you need to go to the fabric store too."

"I'll probably get fabric at my aunt Rebecca's shop in Schellberg," Katy said.

"Ah, yes." Mrs. Graber nodded wisely. "You work for her

sometimes, don't you? And she pays you with store credit instead of an hourly wage."

Was there anything Mrs. Graber didn't already know? Katy felt as though someone had peeled back her skin and showed this woman her insides.

Mrs. Graber went on. "She has a nice shop, but I couldn't find anything heavy enough for curtains."

Just then, they passed the sewing section of the craft store. A bold purple fabric — what Aunt Rebecca called a tone-on-tone — caught Katy's eye. She came to a stop and called, "Dad! Dad, wait a minute!"

Dad turned back, nearly bumping into another shopper. After excusing himself, he bustled to Katy's side. "What?"

"Look at this. Isn't it pretty?" Katy held the loose end of the bolt out. The light caught the fabric, bringing the large checked purple-on-purple pattern into view. Katy had never seen a prettier fabric. Oh, why couldn't Aunt Rebecca have this fabric in her store?

Dad shrugged. "I suppose. It's awfully purple."

"I really, really like it." Katy smoothed her hand over the fabric. Her favorite flowers in the summertime were pansies. The fabric's rich color closely matched their velvety purple petals. Somewhere in the back of her mind she carried a memory of her mother planting pansies along the east side of the house. Or at least she thought she did. The memories were so fuzzy, sometimes it was hard to know if they were real or imagined. She smoothed the fabric again.

"You think Gramma Ruthie would want *that* on her dinner table?" Dad sounded doubtful.

Katy's shoulders sagged. She hadn't been thinking of Gramma Ruthie's dinner table when she spotted the fabric.

She wanted a dress made of this fabric. But she wasn't buying for herself, she was buying for others. And Dad obviously missed the hint that she'd like him to buy it for her.

Mrs. Graber stepped forward. "I think Kathleen is right. It's lovely." She slipped the bolt from its slot on the shelf. "Where is the cutting table? I believe I'm going to take a length of this for a dress."

Katy nearly swallowed her tongue. Mrs. Graber intended to make a dress out of Katy's fabric? Silently, Katy pointed toward the cutting table. She watched the store worker measure the fabric, cut off a length, and fold it into a square. The worker placed the fabric into Mrs. Graber's waiting hands.

Mrs. Graber flashed a bright smile. "I'm ready to pay now."

Katy trailed behind her dad and Mrs. Graber on the way to the checkout counters. She couldn't take her eyes off the neatly folded square of bold purple fabric. She had to be nice to Mrs. Graber — she *had* to — but her biggest test would come the day that woman showed up wearing a dress made of Katy's chosen fabric.

Chapter Eleven

When Katy, Dad, and Mrs. Graber finished shopping, they headed to the food court for lunch. Katy loved eating at the Chinese place in the food court. Dad didn't care for it, but it didn't matter because he could go a few booths over and order a double cheeseburger, fries, and a root beer. Then they were both happy.

Katy ordered cashew chicken with vegetable fried rice and an eggroll. Dad followed Mrs. Graber to a pizzeria, and they both ordered double slices of cheese pizza. Watching Dad bite into a slice of pizza instead of his usual cheeseburger took a bit of the enjoyment away from Katy's dinner, but no one would have guessed. She smiled and chatted, entertaining both adults the way a proper hostess would. Each time Dad gave Katy a little smiling nod of approval, she shut down her conscience and congratulated herself on an act well performed. *Dad 1 – Katy 3.*

She dozed on the way home, awaking with a jolt when Dad turned off the car's ignition. They all climbed out of the car, and Mrs. Graber gave Katy a hug. Taken by surprise, Katy automatically hugged her back.

"You have a good Christmas, Kathleen," Mrs. Graber said.

"Thanks, I will."

Mrs. Graber turned to Dad and held out her hand. He took it. "You too, Samuel." They stood for quite a while, looking at one another without saying anything. Katy squirmed, her gaze bouncing around the yard to keep from watching Dad. Didn't he know he was making a fool out of himself?

Finally, Dad let go of the woman's hand with a sigh that created a wispy cloud. "Well, you better go in before you catch cold." Still looking at Mrs. Graber, he added, "Katy, grab our bags out of the backseat, and let's go."

In the truck, Dad sighed again. Katy nearly growled in irritation. Was he actually *moping*? He was taking this too far. Before Katy could ask if he intended to just sit here in the truck in front of Grampa and Gramma's house, he glanced at his wristwatch. "Hmm, it's only two o'clock. Should we go by Rebecca's so you can find some material to make those placemats for Gramma?"

Her heart lifted. His willingness to take her surely meant he'd set aside his thoughts of Mrs. Graber. "Sure!"

Cars filled the area right in front of Aunt Rebecca's shop, so Dad had to park down the block. The shop bustled with almost as much activity as the mall in Salina, but Katy took Dad's hand and tugged him to the section of the store that housed bolts of fabrics. After a few minutes of browsing, she pointed out a pale green cotton fabric with gold fern leaves. "What do you think of this?"

"That looks a lot more like something your grandma would like than that purple."

Katy almost bristled. *Is that how you'll feel about it when you see it being worn by your girlfriend?* It still rankled her that Mrs. Graber had purchased the purple fabric. It would serve her right if Dad told her the dress was ugly. She smiled, imagining it.

"So is that what you're going to get?"

Dad's question brought Katy back to the present. She snatched the bolt from the rack. "Yes, I'll need thread and batting too."

"Well, hurry up, huh?" Dad looked around the shop and shook his head. "This place is so crowded, it's making me nervous. I think I'll wait in the truck."

Katy laughed. "Okay." Dad charged out of the shop, and Katy quickly selected a spool of thread and a package of quilt batting. She got in line behind two women and chatted with them while she waited for her turn to have her fabric cut. One of Katy's twin cousins, Lola, worked the cutting table. When Katy handed her the bolt of fabric, she crinkled her nose.

"This looks like something an old lady would like."

Katy said, "It's to make placemats for Gramma Ruthie."

"Oh, well then I guess it's okay. How much do you need?"

Katy told her and watched Lola measure the fabric. Lola picked up the scissors and snipped through the fern leaves. "Are you going to the popcorn-stringing party at the Brauns' tonight?"

Dad had told Caleb Katy couldn't go with him since they planned to do their Christmas shopping. But since they'd returned early, that excuse was gone. Katy didn't know what she would do. Rather than answering Lola's question, she asked one of her own. "Are you and Lori going?"

Lola shrugged. "I don't know. Depends on when we finish up here and how tired we are. We're not used to working in the shop, you know—that's usually your job."

Katy decided not to respond to Lola's dig. Aunt Rebecca had given Katy the Saturday off to do her Christmas shopping, so Lola had no reason to complain.

Lola continued. "Lori really wants to go, though. Mom usually doesn't let us go to the community parties yet—she says we're still too young." Lola made a face. "But she said this one was okay since some of the popcorn strings will go on the cedar tree outside the church for the Christmas Eve service."

Katy almost hoped the twins wouldn't go to the party. If they went, they'd be sure to tell Caleb she'd been in the shop. They couldn't keep anything secret.

Lola leaned closer and made a face. "It's been really busy today—even people from Salina. Mom's pre-made baby quilts and wall hangings are almost all gone. I guess everybody's doing last-minute stuff before Christmas."

"I guess so," Katy agreed.

Lola's expression turned scheming. "Speaking of Christmas, did you get anything for Mrs. Graber?"

Katy frowned. "Why would I?"

"Well, she's gonna be your stepmother. You want to get on her good side, right? So did you get her something good?"

Katy began folding the fabric Lola had cut. "No, I didn't get her anything. I don't know her that well. And you don't *know* that she's going to be my stepmother."

Lola snickered. "Oh, Katy, everyone in town knows your dad's gonna ask her to marry him. The deacons approved it, so it's gonna happen."

Without answering, Katy grabbed her thread, batting, and fabric and headed to the cash register. *Everybody's going to be wrong this time,* she vowed. *My dad's not marrying Mrs. Graber ... or anybody else.*

After signing a credit slip for Aunt Rebecca, Katy hurried to the truck. Lola's comment about the deacons approving Dad to court Mrs. Graber replayed in her head, and she stomped her feet hard against the walkway. Dad had said he was going to ask permission, but he hadn't told her he'd received it. Why hadn't he said anything about it? She should have known before Lola found out. Dad probably told Gramma Ruthie, who told Aunt Rebecca, who told someone else, and Lola or Lori overheard. Those girls were always listening in when they shouldn't be. Katy loved her cousins, but sometimes they aggravated her. Like now.

She slid into the truck's cab, slammed the door, and said, "All right. I'm done."

Dad started the engine without a word. Katy's tongue twitched to ask Dad if he'd been given permission by the deacons to court Mrs. Graber. She also wanted to know if he'd bought the widow a Christmas gift. But she didn't ask. She was afraid of the answers. Dad wasn't exactly demonstrative—most of the time his gifts were practical. If he bought Mrs. Graber something better than a new iron or a pair of gloves, it would make Katy mad. So she steamed quietly while they drove out to the dairy.

When Dad pulled onto the yard, he said, "Our day ended earlier than I thought it would."

"Yeah, I know." Katy sighed. "Bummer." The school word slipped out unexpectedly.

Dad's forehead crinkled. "Bummer?"

"I mean, I'm sorry we didn't have more time." Katy began gathering up the bags that cluttered the truck floor. "I thought we'd spend most of the day at the mall. But we didn't." She tried to keep the resentment out of her voice, but she wasn't sure she succeeded.

Dad nodded slowly. "No, we didn't. So that means you could go to that popcorn-stringing party if you wanted to."

Katy paused with her hands full of bags. "But Caleb's not coming over. If I'm not here, you'll have to do the milking all by yourself."

"Every now and then it's all right. The cows can wait their turns. If you want to go to the party, I'll take you over to the Brauns'."

Katy nibbled her lower lip and considered going. All of her friends would be there, including Annika. But Caleb would be there, and he'd probably do something to annoy her. He usually did. *I wish Bryce could come* ... She pushed that thought away. Piling the bags in her lap, she made a decision.

"How about if I stay and help with the milking, then we string popcorn for our tree?"

Dad's lips quirked into a funny little grin. "You'd rather stay here than be with your friends?"

"With all the homework and school stuff"—*and you spending time with Mrs. Graber*—"we haven't had much time together. I think I'd rather just stay home with you. I'll go to the community New Year's Eve party with my friends."

Dad's grin grew. "Well, all right then. That sounds fine, Katy-girl."

"And," Katy went on, ideas building, "I'll fix us a special supper—all of your favorites. We'll make it a real party."

"Are you sure you want to go to all that trouble?"

"It's not so much trouble. Honest. Especially since I didn't work at Aunt Rebecca's shop today. I'm not tired, and I've got lots of time."

"Well then . . ." Dad rubbed his chin. "What if we made it a bigger party?"

Katy tipped her head to the side. "How?"

"We haven't had Grampa and Gramma over for a while. I could drive back into town and invite them. Should we ask them to join us?"

For several seconds Katy sat without saying anything. She didn't mind having Grampa and Gramma out—they were family. But if they came, Mrs. Graber would come too. It would be rude to leave her behind. And if Mrs. Graber came, Dad would only pay attention to her.

She swallowed hard. "If that's what you want . . . okay." She opened the truck door.

"Katy?"

She turned back, hoping Dad would say, "I changed my mind. Let's just have that party by ourselves." But he said, "Should I see if Gramma Ruthie will bring dessert?"

"Sure, Dad." *Dad 2 – . . .* She bumped the door closed with her hip, hugged the packages to her aching chest, and ran for the house.

Chapter Twelve

After dinner, Grampa Ben advised Katy to stack the dishes in the sink and wash them later. "That way we can get to popcorn stringing now."

Katy looked at Dad. He didn't like unwashed dishes in the sink, so she always cleaned up immediately after meals. But he was wearing the silly grin he always put on when Mrs. Graber was around and nodded in agreement. "That sounds fine. Katy-girl, get out the big kettle, and I'll fetch the popcorn from the cellar." He disappeared through the doorway leading to the storage space below the kitchen.

Katy pulled their largest soup kettle from its spot under the worktable and then removed the jug of oil from the shelf. While she heated the oil in the bottom of the kettle, Mrs. Graber and Gramma Ruthie cleared the table and stacked the dishes in the sink. Dad trotted into the kitchen with the bag of popcorn kernels in his hand and a huge smile on his face.

"Here you go." He plopped the bag onto the corner of the stove.

"How many batches, Dad?" Katy measured out the

kernels and poured them into the hot oil. They bounced like BBs in the iron kettle, making it sound like they were already starting to pop.

"Hmm, good question." He looked at Grampa. "How many do you think, Dad?"

"Start with four," Grampa suggested, "and we can pop more if we need it. 'Course ..." He chuckled. "We'll be eatin' some too, so maybe you better start with five."

Katy wrinkled her nose. "Grampa, we need dry popcorn for stringing. Dry popcorn tastes terrible and sticks to your teeth!"

Grampa crossed the floor to tap Katy's nose with his finger. "Then make the first batch for eatin' an' the rest for stringin'. Even though I had two servings of your grandma's peach cobbler, I've got plenty of room for popcorn." He patted his belly.

Katy laughed. "Okay, Grampa Ben."

Mrs. Graber turned from the sink and wiped her hands on the apron she'd tied around her waist. Katy prided herself that she hadn't even blinked when the woman took it from the hook behind the door as if she owned the kitchen. "Kathleen, would you like my help?"

"Oh, no." Katy smiled sweetly and continued shaking the pot to heat the kernels. "I've been doing this for years, so I'm just fine, but thank you."

"Well, then," Gramma Ruthie said, "since Katy has the popcorn popping under control, let's go sit in the living room and talk."

"Or ..." Dad stepped forward, rubbing his chin with his finger. "You haven't ever seen the house, have you, Rosemary?"

Katy gulped.

"Not the whole house." Mrs. Graber sounded hopeful.

"Then let's take a quick, well, tour." Dad laughed like he'd made a joke. Katy resisted rolling her eyes. "You've seen the kitchen and living room, but you haven't been upstairs."

Don't you take her in my *room!* Katy speeded up the stirring, flicking kernels against the sides of the kettle. How could she keep them downstairs? "This popcorn's about ready to pop, Dad. Are you sure there's time?"

Dad laughed again. "The house isn't that big, Katy. We'll be back in time to sample the popcorn." He held out his arm toward the living room. "This way, Rosemary."

Gramma and Grampa followed Dad and Mrs. Graber, leaving Katy alone. *Dad 3 – Katy 3.* She was losing ground fast. She tipped her head, straining to hear what was going on upstairs, but the popcorn began to pop. She slapped the lid on the kettle. The explosion of popcorn kernels filled the room and made it impossible to hear anything else, but she imagined the four adults going through the three upstairs rooms.

Katy didn't mind them being in Dad's bedroom, but the other two rooms she'd claimed as hers. She used the smallest bedroom as a sewing room. The only private item in there was her sewing machine, which had been her mother's. She didn't want Mrs. Graber touching it. She also didn't like the idea of them all wandering through her bedroom, examining her things. Would Mrs. Graber laugh at the stuffed bear on her bed or the collection of dolls that sat in a neat row on the shelf above her desk?

The kettle fell silent, just a few late pops echoing under

the lid, so Katy lifted the kettle from the stove. As she poured the white, fluffy popped corn into a big bowl, the sounds of footsteps on the stairs and voices carried into the kitchen. Grampa and Dad came in first followed by Gramma and Mrs. Graber. Dad and Grampa moved to the table to sneak a few pieces of popcorn, but the two women dashed to the back door.

Katy tried to peer around Dad and Grampa to see what Gramma and Mrs. Graber were doing, but the men blocked her view. Then the back door hinges squeaked and cold air whisked into the kitchen, which meant someone went outside.

Katy looked at Dad. "Is Mrs. Graber leaving?" She hoped she sounded dismayed rather than eager.

Dad shrugged, munching a piece of popcorn. "Oh, she just needs to run to the car for a minute. She'll be back." He rubbed his hands together. "This popcorn needs butter and salt. I'll get it."

The evening crawled by. Katy usually loved the smell of popcorn, loved time with Gramma Ruthie and Grampa Ben, loved talking and laughing around the table while they worked on a project together. But tonight — even though she smiled and talked and laughed as if she was having fun — she couldn't relax. While she laughed, her stomach jumped in apprehension. While her hands pushed a needle through snowy puffs of popped corn, her thoughts bounced here and there. *Why did Mrs. Graber have to run to her car after being upstairs? Why did she and Dad keep giving each other secretive looks across the table?* When would this evening end so Katy could go upstairs, shut herself away, and record her frustrations in her journal?

By ten o'clock, a misshapen pile of popcorn strings filled the center of the dining room table. Dad sat back, admired the heap, and laughed. "Katy-girl, we better get our tree up quickly so we can move these strings off the table. Otherwise, we won't have any place to sit and eat!"

"When are you getting your tree?" Mrs. Graber asked.

"Probably tomorrow afternoon, after lunch." Dad flicked a glance at Katy. "Is that okay with you, Katy-girl?"

One of their Christmas traditions was walking out into the pasture, cutting down a wild cedar tree, and hauling it home to cover with handmade decorations and long strings of popcorn. She always looked forward to "Christmas tree day," but now she held her breath. Would Dad invite Mrs. Graber to be a part of the Katy-and-Dad tradition? She wasn't sure she could act happy if that woman intruded on such a special time.

"I—I guess so. I had hoped to maybe invite Annika over to make Christmas candies ..."

Dad scratched his chin. "Well, we could get the tree Monday, if that works better for you."

Mrs. Graber smiled. "You two have fun decorating your tree, whether it's tomorrow or Monday." She toyed with a string of popcorn. "I'll be driving back to Meschke after service tomorrow, but I'll be thinking of you."

If Mrs. Graber wasn't going to be around, then Katy didn't need to worry about her intruding. She said quickly, "Annika and I can always make candy later in the week, Dad. If you want to hunt up a tree tomorrow afternoon, that'll be fine."

"Oh, good." Dad pushed away from the table, and the

other grown-ups stood too. "Then we can get this popcorn off the table and onto a tree, where it belongs."

Grampa, Gramma, and Mrs. Graber put on their coats and headed for the back door. As they passed the sink, Gramma stopped and looked at Katy. "Katy-girl, should I stay and help you get those dishes out of the way? It's late, and you need to get to bed soon."

Katy flipped her hands to shoo the others toward the door. "I can take care of those dishes just fine by myself. And I won't oversleep tomorrow — I promise." She smiled. "Good-night. Thank you for the help stringing popcorn. I'll see you in service tomorrow."

Dad closed the door behind the others then turned to face Katy. "Hand me a dish towel, and I'll dry for you."

Katy stared at Dad. "Are you sure?" Dad hated drying dishes. He said it was more boring than counting cows.

"You'll have to get up early to help with the milking. It's only fair I stay up late with you and help with your chore."

Katy decided not to argue. "Okay." She grabbed a towel from a drawer. "Here you go."

Outside the window, the black sky glittered with stars. Inside, the scents of popcorn and soap fragranced the room. The soft splash of her hands in the dishwater and the squeak of the towel on clean dishes created a homey mood. Katy giggled.

"What's funny?" Dad placed a plate in the cupboard.

"Nothing's funny. I'm just happy."

"Oh?" Dad leaned his hip against the counter and picked up a bowl. "Why?"

"In a few more days, it'll be Christmas. Tomorrow we get to put up our tree. And right now it's just you and me in our house. I feel ..." Katy searched for the right word. "Peaceful."

Dad chuckled. "Peaceful is a good way to feel."

Katy added, "It was fun to have Gramma and Grampa out, but I like it when it's just us too." Would he understand what she was trying to say?

Dad gave Katy's shoulder a quick squeeze. "I like it too, Katy. You're growing up so fast. It won't be long and you'll have a house and family of your own. But for now ..." He grinned and picked up a handful of silverware from the drainer. "We can enjoy our time together."

Katy smiled. *Dad 3 – Katy 4 ...* The count didn't matter nearly as much as the warm feelings filling her inside.

He looked at the remaining dishes in the drainer. "You know what? Those can dry on their own, and you can put them away in the morning. It's late. Let's go have our Bible reading, then we can go on up to bed."

Katy took the towel from Dad and draped it across the dripping dishes. She followed him to the living room and sat at the opposite end of the sofa. He opened his time-worn Bible and began reading from Psalms, a familiar passage. She closed her eyes as she listened, Dad's soft voice like a lullaby to her. When he finished the passage, he bowed his head and offered a short prayer. Katy echoed his "Amen."

"Lights," he said, and Katy flipped the switch on the lamp next to the sofa. Dad pulled the string for the overhead light, and then they moved up the stairs. When they reached the landing, Dad flashed a quick smile. "Goodnight, Katy-girl. Remember to set your alarm so we don't keep the cows waiting."

"Yes, Dad. See you in the morning." It felt so good to be relaxed and at peace with Dad. The good feeling followed her into her room where she changed into her nightgown and brushed out her hair for bed. But when she carried her dress to the closet to put it in the dirty clothes basket, the peace shattered.

Her closet door, which she always kept closed, stood slightly ajar. Her heart doubled its tempo. Katy opened the door slowly, her eyes scanning every detail of the closet. Shoes side by side on the floor beside the wicker basket that held her dirty clothes, a box of discarded toys pushed into the far corner. Nothing disturbed on the floor. But then she scowled. Her dresses were crunched together. She always left a little space between them so they wouldn't get wrinkled. *Someone* had been messing with her clothes!

Katy started to charge across the landing to ask Dad if he'd been in her closet, but a glance at the clock stopped her. It was after eleven already. Dad had been up since before five that morning. She shouldn't bother him.

She closed the closet door with a soft click and crossed to her desk. If someone had peeked in her closet, had they looked through her drawers too? With shaking hands, she eased open the drawer that held the spiral notebook where she recorded her thoughts. Then she nearly sagged in relief. The journal was pressed in the corner with her pencil sticking out between pages, just the way she'd left it.

Katy pulled out the notebook and opened it flat on her desk. She picked up the pencil and wrote, "Someone got into my closet and rearranged my dresses. I bet it was Mrs. Graber. She's nosy, finding out all kinds of details about me and then snooping through my room. I'm glad she's

going back to Meschke tomorrow, and I hope she decides
not to come back. I don't need a snoopy, nosy woman in
MY house, going through MY things, and taking over MY
dad's attention and affection."

Katy expended every angry thought she'd kept bottled
inside all day. Then, when the page was full, she tore it
loose and started to shred it. But her hands froze on the
paper. No, she wouldn't tear it up. She folded it in half and
slipped it into the journal as a page holder.

She put the notebook back in the drawer and quickly
crawled into bed. Tugging the blankets to her chin, she
smiled. If Mrs. Graber snooped again, maybe she'd find
that page. Then she'd know how Katy felt about her. And
if she was smart, she'd walk out of Katy's house and never
come back.

Chapter Thirteen

Katy fidgeted on the bench as she waited for the Christmas Eve service to begin. Sometimes she battled boredom during the weekly worship with its hymns, long sermons, Bible reading, and prayers. But the Christmas Eve service was never boring.

Strange how much more interesting she found it when there was little difference between a Christmas Eve service and a regular worship service in content. The women sat on one side, men on the other, like always. The deacons read the Bible, the song leader directed a few hymns, and one of the deacons delivered a long sermon, just like a regular service.

But on Christmas Eve, instead of turning on the overhead electric lights, candles glowed on the windowsills. A towering Christmas tree, its branches heavy with strings of popcorn and cranberries, filled the room with the scent of pine. They sang Christmas hymns such as "Silent Night" and "O Little Town of Bethlehem" in German rather than English, and somehow the music made Katy's chest feel both full and light as air.

She sat beside Gramma Ruthie and listened as one of the deacons opened his Bible and read the familiar Christmas story. Even though she'd heard it every year since she could remember, she never grew tired of it. She closed her eyes and imagined the scene in Bethlehem: the star, the stable, the little baby wrapped in tattered cloths. Tears pricked her eyes when she imagined the young mother cradling her newborn son, not knowing what the future would hold for this innocent, tiny babe.

When the deacon closed the Bible, the song leader went forward and led the congregation in "Hark! the Herald Angels Sing." Katy wanted to sing at the top of her voice, from the very center of her soul. But she kept her volume even with the others rather than stand out. Singing louder than everyone would be interpreted as prideful, and she couldn't be prideful. Especially at Christmas.

A deacon closed the service in prayer, then he smiled and held his arms wide. "Let us retire to the basement for a time of fellowship and refreshment." Younger kids whooped and were immediately shushed by their parents, but then laughter rang, and everyone crowded toward the stairway that led to the large room beneath the church.

Tables and folding chairs filled the center of the floor, and tables along the back wall held homemade candies, cookies, and a variety of rich breads. People formed a line. Just like always, the fellowship's eldest members went first, followed by families with small children, and finally everyone else. Since Katy was neither elderly nor a small child, she held back and ended up nearly at the end of the line. Gramma Ruthie could have been at the front with Grampa Ben, but she stayed with Katy.

A spicy fragrance reached Katy's nose, and she nudged Gramma. "Did Mr. Plett bring apple cider?"

Gramma's eyes crinkled with her grin. "Doesn't he always bring it for Christmas?"

Katy licked her lips in anticipation. Mr. Plett made the best apple cider she'd ever tasted. Everyone speculated about what he put in it to give it such a sweet yet tart flavor, but no one knew the secret. "Ohhhh, I can't wait! Christmas isn't Christmas without it."

Gramma nodded her head in agreement. "But he's getting older — he's almost eighty already. He needs to teach one of his sons how to make it, or when he's gone no one will taste it again."

Katy didn't like to think about people being gone. She changed the subject. "Are you and Grampa Ben opening your presents tonight after the service, or are you waiting until tomorrow?"

Gramma laughed softly. "Now, Katy-girl, your grandpa and I gave up gift-buying for each other a long time ago. What do a couple of old folks like us need, anyway?"

Katy and Gramma Ruthie continued chatting while the line inched forward, and they finally reached the food table. Just as Katy's hands closed around a plate, someone tapped her shoulder. She glanced back to find Annika.

"The young people are sitting on the stairs. So after you get your plate, join us there, okay?" Annika's eyes sparkled beneath her cap.

Katy could never figure out why Annika, who spent her days in a big family with lots of people around, was always so ready to join a group. Katy would have preferred a quiet corner with just her friend, but she wouldn't spoil Annika's fun. "Okay. I'll be there in a minute."

She filled her white ceramic plate with all the goodies it could hold, accepted a tin cup of apple cider, then worked her way through the crowded basement room to the staircase. Annika had saved her a few inches of space on a lower step, so Katy wiggled into position with the others. The knees of the person behind her pressed between her shoulder blades, and Annika's elbow squashed her into the corner. Katy decided standing would be more comfortable, so she moved to the floor.

Leaning against the wall, she faced the young people from the congregation. Caleb's red hair glowed like a beacon, but she tried to avoid making eye contact with him. When her gaze skittered sideways to avoid Caleb, it collided with Annika's sister Taryn and her beau. The pair snuggled as close as they could get, teasingly feeding each other small pieces of pumpkin bread. Their behavior reminded Katy of Dad and Mrs. Graber, and she quickly looked away only to find Caleb staring right at her.

"Hey, Katydid, did your dad let you open that package already?" Caleb's voice carried over the others.

Katy frowned. "What package?"

"The one that came in the mail. I saw him pick it up at the post office when I was getting my family's mail."

"I don't know what you're talking about." Katy lifted a square of sticky fudge between her finger and thumb and nibbled the edge.

Caleb grinned. "It was a good-sized one. Mailed from out of town."

Katy nearly rolled her eyes. Of course, it was mailed

from out of town. Anyone who lived *in* town would just hand a package to her rather than waste postage mailing it.

"It had Christmas stickers all over it," Caleb went on, his voice growing louder.

The other conversations seemed to lose steam. Everyone looked from Caleb to Katy. One of the other boys said, "What had Christmas stickers all over it?"

"The package that came for Katy." Caleb pointed at her with a stick of peppermint. "A big one from out of town."

"Oh, yeah?" Lori, Katy's cousin, perked up. "Who was it from, Caleb?"

"I don't think it had a name or return address on it," Caleb said. "I didn't see one."

Lori looked at her twin sister, Lola. "Did we get any Christmas packages from out of town?"

Lola shook her head.

Lori pursed her lips. "Then it can't be from a relative, or we would've gotten something too. Who else would send Katy a Christmas package?"

Annika shot a defensive look at the twins. "Lots of people. Katy has friends in Salina. Probably one of them sent a Christmas gift to her."

Katy's ears started to heat up. She hoped the package hadn't come from Shelby or one of the other girls from school. She hadn't gotten anything for them. It would be too embarrassing to receive something without giving something in return.

Lola made a face. "Don't be silly. If they were going to give Katy a present, they'd have done it before they left school. They wouldn't *mail* it."

"How do you know?" Annika glared at the younger girl.

"Maybe they'd mail something — especially if they didn't have it ready before school let out. You don't know those kids, so you don't know what they'd do."

"Well, *you* don't know them either," Lori said.

Lola folded her arms over her chest and huffed. "I think it's silly. Nobody mails a Christmas package unless they can't see the person for the holiday. Unless ..." Suddenly Lola's eyebrows flew high. She giggled.

"What?" Lori asked.

Lola sent her twin a sly look. "Unless it's like a secret admirer kind of thing. Someone who likes her but wants to be anonymous." The twins put their heads together and giggled.

A horrible thought entered Katy's head. What if Caleb had mailed her a present? It was just the sort of thing he'd do — send it through the mail rather than hand it to her and risk having it rejected. And then bring it up to see how she'd react.

"You're being ridiculous now," Annika said, and for a moment Katy wondered if she'd spoken her thought out loud.

Then one of the older kids leaned forward and joined the conversation. "No, think about it: Katy goes to that school in Salina. Maybe there's a kid there who decided he or she wanted to give Katy a present. But the kid didn't know whether she was allowed to accept one. So instead of making her uncomfortable by giving it to her there, they mailed it instead."

Caleb snorted. "How funny! Katydid with a secret admirer!" She hoped that meant Caleb wasn't the gift-sender. He laughed loudly, and a few others snickered.

Could Bryce have sent her a Christmas present? Katy's stomach swirled in a funny way — part apprehension, part anticipation.

"So who do you think it is, Katy?" Caleb called, still chuckling. "Do you have any guesses?"

As if she'd tell Caleb about Bryce! Katy pushed off from the wall, ready to tell Caleb and everybody else to mind their own business. But Dad came around the corner, interrupting.

"Katy, are you ready to go?"

Although Katy usually wanted to be one of the last ones to leave the Christmas Eve fellowship, she discovered she was ready. "Yes, Dad." She handed Annika her empty plate. "Would you put that in the kitchen for me?"

"Sure, Katy," Annika agreed. She lowered her voice to a whisper. "Be sure to tell me who that package is from!"

The kids scooted to the edges of the staircase to allow Katy and her dad through. Their whispers and laughter followed Katy around the corner to the cloakrooms. When Katy and Dad were in the truck, she said, "Dad, Caleb said you picked up a package at the post office that had Christmas stickers all over it."

Dad rubbed his lips together. "Yes, I did."

"Was it addressed to me?"

The cab of the truck was dark, but Katy thought she saw her dad grimace. "Yes, it was."

"Why didn't you give it to me?"

Dad turned the steering wheel and angled the truck onto the road that led home. He gave her a lopsided grin. "Well, Katy-girl, it's a Christmas package. So I was saving it for Christmas."

"Are we going to open our packages tonight?"

Dad's grin grew. "Don't we always open our packages on Christmas Eve night?"

Yes, they did, because Christmas morning they had to see to the cows. The cows didn't stop producing milk just because it was a holiday. Katy settled back in the seat, her stomach whirling in eagerness. Oh, how she hoped the gift was from Bryce!

Chapter Fourteen

Katy came around the corner from hanging up her coat and caught Dad peeking under the tree. "What are you doing?"

He straightened and grinned sheepishly. "There isn't anything under here with my name on it."

She laughed. "As if I'd put anything for you out early! You snoop."

"I do not."

"Yes, you do. I've caught you shaking boxes before."

Dad gave her an innocent look. "I only did that once."

Katy laughed again. "Stay here." She started back toward the staircase. "I'll go get your present." She clattered up the stairs, pulled both of Dad's presents from underneath the bed, then raced back down in time to see Dad slide a brown paper–wrapped gift decorated with bright wreath, star, and holly stickers under the tree. Her hands shook as she knelt to put Dad's gifts beside the mysterious package. Although she wanted to snatch up that package and tear off the paper, she told Dad, "You first. Which one do you want?"

Dad held out his hands. "The biggest one, of course."

Katy giggled and handed Dad the larger of the two packages. With a big grin, he peeled back the green and red striped paper and popped loose the tape. Katy clasped her hands beneath her chin, eager for his reaction. She'd purchased something completely impractical, and she hoped he would like it.

Dad pried off the top of the box then sat staring at the contents with a dumbfounded look on his face. "Well, I'll be."

Katy smiled. "Do you like it?"

Dad carefully lifted out the gift and held it at arm's length. "Well, sure I do, Katy-girl, but ... what is it?"

Katy couldn't help laughing. "It's a seat cover for the truck!"

"A what?"

She took it from him and unfolded it, revealing a heavy, ribbed seat cover of black rubber. Although the store carried several colors and patterns, including purple polka dots and yellow and green animal print, she'd chosen black because it would meet the approval of the deacons. "You put this over your seat in the truck. It's cushioned so it'll be comfortable, and it'll protect you from the seat being either too hot or too cold."

"Well, I'll be," Dad repeated. He squished the thick rubber and chuckled. "I sure wouldn't have thought of buying something like that for myself. It's a dandy gift, Katy. Thank you."

She beamed at him. "You're welcome."

He set the cover aside, gave it a pat, then reached under the tree to pull out a box about the size of a cereal box. "Here you go."

Katy almost dropped it when she took it. It weighed more than she expected. She placed it on her lap and carefully removed the paper, trying to keep from tearing it. She chuckled when the box proved to be a corn flakes box. Dad didn't waste things. He'd secured the top flaps with at least a dozen strips of tape, and it took some doing to work all the tape loose. Finally, she got it open. She tipped the box, and three books spilled across the floor. She gasped. "Dad!"

His eyes sparkled. "So you like them?"

"Oh, I do!" Katy scooped up the first of two diaries. The cover showed a smattering of bright flowers, similar to her backpack. A flap held the book closed, and a little lock secured the flap in place. The second one had a lock too, but the cover was solid blue with thin green stripes. The third book was a fat thesaurus. Mr. Gorsky had a row of them on the bookshelf in the English room, but Katy had never imagined owning one herself.

She giggled with delight, partly over the wonderful presents, but partly because Dad had never bought her anything so personal. She reached out and hugged his neck. "Oh, this is so much better than a new iron! Thank you."

"You're welcome." Dad patted her back. "Figured anybody who liked to write as much as you do should have a special place to record your writings." He chuckled again. "And that thesaurus should give you some fancy words to record."

Katy made a neat stack of the books with the thesaurus on the bottom and the flowered diary on top. She fingered the little lock on the flowered diary, and her heart pattered in her chest. Now that she could lock her words away from any other eyes, she'd never have to tear up another page of writing. She could write and write without worry. "These are the best presents ever."

Dad grinned. "Good. Now, is there another one for me?"

Katy burst out laughing. The only time Dad acted like a kid was at Christmas. She loved it. If only Christmas could last forever. She handed him the second package and watched him open it. Even though it wasn't very personal — a pair of sturdy work gloves and a new scarf — he thanked her enthusiastically. Practical gifts made sense there on the farm.

Dad gave her a second gift, which turned out to be three ballpoint pens in fun colors: green, purple, and red. "Oh, Dad, thanks! I love them." She shook her head in wonder. What had gotten into Dad this year?

"And one more . . ." Dad slid the package with the Christmas stickers out from the under the tree and placed it in Katy's lap.

Katy examined the handwriting on the brown paper. Neatly printed, almost block letters. She frowned. She'd seen Bryce's masculine, messy scrawl on lots of flow charts in debate. This writing didn't resemble his at all. So it probably wasn't from Bryce. She fought a wave of disappointment and looked at Dad. "Who's it from?"

Dad propped his hands behind him and leaned back. "Open it and find out."

Katy took as much care removing the simple brown paper as she had the pretty paper from her other gifts. Under the brown paper, she discovered a plain white box. No tape held it closed, so it took no effort to remove the top. Inside, layers of white tissue paper hid the present from view. Katy pushed the tissue paper aside. She stared at the gift for several startled seconds, then her gaze bounced up to meet Dad's. A silly grin creased his face. Katy's stomach clenched. The present wasn't a surprise to him.

"Well, take it out and hold it up. I want to see what it will look like on you," he said.

But Katy didn't reach for it. The dress, sewn from the purple fabric she'd seen in the mall, begged to be picked up, shaken out, and admired. But she couldn't do it. Why had Mrs. Graber made this?

"Katy?" Dad sounded puzzled.

She looked at him.

"What's wrong?"

She doesn't have the right to sew for me. She's not my mother. She's not anyone to me! The ugly thoughts stayed inside her head.

Dad tugged the box onto the floor between them and pulled the dress from the box. A second dress—a familiar one from Katy's closet—lay folded in the bottom of the box. Dad said, "Rosemary wanted it to be a surprise, so she borrowed one of your dresses instead of asking you for your size. She had to sew fast to get it done in time to mail it to you." Dad's soft voice held a note of confusion. "I thought you liked this purple material."

Katy stared with longing at the dress. She loved the purple material. The dress was beautiful—the most beautiful dress she'd ever had, just as she'd known it would be when she spotted the fabric. But how could she wear it, knowing Mrs. Graber had made it for her? How could she accept it after her mean thoughts about the woman buying

her fabric? She'd feel like a hypocrite, wearing that dress ...
Tears threatened.

"I—I do like the purple material. It's just ..." She swallowed, trying hard not to cry.

"It's just what?" Dad stood up and held the dress by its shoulders. The lovely purple-on-purple squares winked in the pale light from the lamp in the corner.

"It's just ... I feel bad."

Dad's forehead crunched. "Why?"

"B-because ..." Katy swallowed again. She didn't dare tell Dad the real reason. "I didn't get anything for her. It—it's not fair to accept a present when I haven't given one."

Dad shook his head. "Well, I don't think she did it to get something from you, Katy."

Oh, yes she did. She did it to win me over. She did it to get my approval. A huge lump filled Katy's throat, preventing her from voicing the thoughts. It was just as well. Dad would only defend Mrs. Graber again, which would make things even worse.

Dad put the dress back in the box, but he didn't fold it. It lay in an accordion-shaped heap. *A dress that pretty shouldn't be wadded up.* Katy's finger itched to fold it neatly. But she still didn't touch it.

Dad said, "If it really bothers you, maybe you could make something for her and mail it. Or give it to her when she comes back in January. It won't matter to her that it's after Christmas."

Katy pushed to her feet and dove into Dad's arms. With her face against his chest, she said, "I'll think about it."

"Good." Dad patted Katy's back. "She helped me pick out your presents this year. She'll be happy to know how much you liked the diaries."

Katy pulled back. "Y-you mean, Mrs. Graber picked those out? It wasn't you?"

Dad laughed. "Well, I paid for them."

Katy didn't smile.

Dad's laughter faded away. "I asked her what she thought you'd like." He shrugged. "I'm not very good at picking out presents, Katy, and I figured she'd know better since she's a ..."

He dropped the final word, leaving Katy wondering if he planned to say *woman* or *mother*. It didn't matter. The joy of receiving the presents disappeared now that she knew Dad hadn't chosen them.

"Why don't you plan on wearing your new dress to dinner at Grampa and Gramma's tomorrow?"

Dad sounded so hopeful, Katy couldn't refuse. "Sure, Dad."

"Good." Dad gave her a quick hug. "Now up to bed. The cows will expect us in the barn at five thirty, just like always. But then we can have a quiet, relaxing morning before we go to Gramma's for lunch."

"Sure, Dad," Katy repeated.

Dad gave her a puzzled look. "Are you okay?"

Once again Katy lied. "I'm fine. It's just been a big day between the church program and opening gifts. I guess I'm a little tired." *And very, very disappointed.*

"Well then, bed for sure. I'll take care of the mess down here ..." He stooped over and began wadding up the discarded wrapping paper.

"Good-night, Dad." Katy turned and headed for the stairs.

"Katy, aren't you going to take your presents up with you?"

She hurried on and pretended she hadn't heard him.

Chapter Fifteen

Katy awakened to the clang of her alarm clock at five on Christmas morning. She slapped the alarm clock into silence and then flopped back onto her pillows. She really wanted to go back to sleep; she'd tossed and turned all night, and her body screamed for rest. But the cows—and Dad—would be waiting for her, so she had to get up.

With a sigh, she tossed aside her covers, tugged on her robe, and headed for the bathroom. When she opened her bedroom door, her toe banged into something in the hallway. Hissing through her teeth, she rubbed her toe and glared at the object blocking the walkway. Her presents. Dad must have put them there when he came up for bed.

Katy bent over and picked up the box Mrs. Graber had used to mail the dress. Dad had put the thesaurus, diaries, and pens on top of it. She plopped the stack on the bed. The books slid sideways to land on the mattress, and the purple dress came into plain view. Katy released a little huff of irritation. The weight of the books had wrinkled the attached modesty cape of the dress. Why had Dad been so careless? Now she'd have to iron the dress before she could wear it.

Well, a little voice in her head chided, *if you'd just carried your presents up yourself, you could have hung the dress in the closet. Don't blame it on Dad.*

She told the voice to shut up. Sighing, she retrieved a hanger from the closet. There would be plenty of time to iron since Dad had said they'd spend a relaxing, quiet morning. She started to sling the dress onto the hanger, but then she stopped and slowly examined the dress from top to bottom. Mrs. Graber had done a nice job. All of the seams were neat, the neckline smooth and round. She'd even tacked down the facing with tiny stitches. Katy usually just ironed the facing down because it was so hard to tack it without wrinkling the fabric. The dress was flawless. How had Mrs. Graber managed to do such a perfect job in so little time?

Releasing another huff of aggravation, Katy stomped to the closet, whacked the hanger onto the rod, and slapped the door closed. Then she put on an old dress, twisted her hair into a braid, and brushed her teeth before going downstairs. Looking through the kitchen window, Katy spotted the light on in the barn. Dad was already out there. She threw her coat over her shoulders and ran across the yard to join him.

Dad waved when she entered the milking room. But they worked without talking, the clank and hum of the machines and the clop of hooves on the concrete floor filling the room with noise. By 7:15, the cows were all in the enclosed corral, mooing for breakfast. Dad fed them while Katy hosed down the milking room walls and floor with a powerful jet stream of water. The mist settled on her hair and clothes, and by the time she finished, she was shivering.

When she joined Dad in the yard, he tugged off his coat

and put it around her. "You're all wet, Katy. You'll catch a cold. C'mon, let's hurry." They trotted to the house, and Dad sent her through the door first. "Go on up and take a hot bath — warm up."

"But what about breakfast?" A bath sounded good, but Dad always liked his breakfast early.

"Breakfast can wait. Go on now."

Katy didn't offer a second argument. Most of the time she bathed quickly so she could get to her chores. Being able to laze in the tub was a rare treat. She added a capful of bubble bath beneath the stream of water. Frothy bubbles burst to life, and she breathed in the scented steam. She filled the tub then climbed through the froth. The bubbles popped and crackled like a bowl of cereal, and she giggled. She slid down until the steaming water lapped gently against her chin.

Closing her eyes, she sighed in contentment. "Ah, Dad just gave me a wonderful gift," she whispered to the empty room. Then she remembered what he'd said last night — that Mrs. Graber had given him the ideas for her gifts — and a snide thought filled her mind: *Had his precious Rosemary told him he needed to let his daughter relax more?*

Once the thought occurred to her, she couldn't even enjoy a leisurely soak. So she quickly washed her hair, dried off, and dressed. Then, with her wet hair trailing down her back, she opened the bathroom door. The tantalizing scent of frying bacon greeted her nose. Frowning, Katy hurried down the stairs and into the kitchen. "Dad, what are you doing?"

Dad stood by the stove with a metal spatula in his

hand. He looked absolutely ridiculous with one of her aprons tied around his waist. If her stomach hadn't been tied in knots, she would have laughed.

Dad grinned at her. "Bath done? Good timing. The bacon's almost done, and then I'll fry some eggs. The toast is already on the table if you want to munch on a piece while I finish over here."

Katy shook her head. What was going on? Dad never cooked. He didn't like to cook. After Katy's mother left their sect, Gramma Ruthie had come out twice a day to fix their breakfast and supper. She and Dad ate sandwiches or canned soup for lunch so Dad didn't have to cook. As soon as Katy was old enough, she took over the cooking. She couldn't remember the last time Dad had fixed something besides a bowl of cereal or a bologna sandwich.

She put her hands on her hips. "Why are you doing this?"

Dad shrugged and pushed the bacon around in the skillet. The grease popped and spattered the stove top. "Consider it a Christmas present."

"But you've never — "

"Get me some paper towels, Katy, would you? I need to drain this bacon."

Katy obediently carried a roll of paper towels to the stove. Dad pulled off several sheets and laid them on the corner of the stove, away from the burner. She watched him transfer the crisp strips from the pan to the stack of paper towels. Confusion clouded her brain. Dad's odd behavior — sending her to take a long bath, cooking breakfast — made her uneasy. Something was up.

"Why don't you let me fry the eggs?" Katy reached for the spatula, but Dad shook his head.

"Nope. Go sit down. I can do it. You want yours over easy, right?"

Katy nodded. A few minutes later, Dad carried two plates of bacon and eggs to the table. Her eggs were well-done instead of over easy, but she didn't say anything. Midway through breakfast, Dad leaned back in his chair and sent a serious look across the table.

"Katy-girl?"

Katy's scalp tingled.

"I plan to make an announcement at Grampa and Gramma's today when the whole family is there. But I want you to hear it first."

The tingle increased. She scratched her head. "What is it?"

Dad's lips twitched into a soft smile. The kind of smile Katy had never seen before on his face. Her heart began thudding so hard she wondered if it moved the cape on her dress. He took a deep breath and said, "I asked Rosemary to become my wife. She said yes. So we'll be getting married the last weekend in February."

For several seconds Katy sat so still she even forgot to breathe. *So that's why Dad fixed me breakfast. To soften me up.* She set her jaw in a firm line. *Well, it isn't going to work!*

Dad went on. "I know this is sudden, but I want you to know that Rosemary is a good woman. She's been a widow for almost as long as I've been a widower. She has children of her own, and I know she'll be a good mother for you. So —"

Katy sucked in a giant breath, pushed her chair back, and jumped up. "But you don't have to do it!" *I'm ahead right now — I have four points to your three. You can't win!*

Dad clacked his mouth shut and stared at her.

"It's okay, Dad. I know I got into trouble, and I know I worried you. But I've been working really hard at showing you I can stay out of trouble. I don't need a mother." Katy's voice rose as words spilled out faster and faster. "You don't have to marry her for me. You don't have to get married at all!"

Dad stood too. He reached across the table and grabbed Katy's shoulder. "I'm not marrying her for you. I'm marrying her because ..." His hand fell away and drifted slowly to the table. "I'm lonely. I want a wife."

Tears filled Katy's eyes. Dad's image swam. "How can you be lonely? You have me ..." Her chest ached so badly it hurt to breathe.

"Katy, Katy ..." Dad sighed. "Sit down, please."

But Katy shook her head.

"All right, then. Stand. But listen to me." Dad pressed both palms to the table and leaned on them. The pose made him looked tired and defeated. "I'm your father and I love you, but loving a child isn't the same as loving a wife."

Katy whisked the tears from her eyes. "I already know that!" She'd never snapped at Dad before. She drew back, expecting him to scold. But he just went on calmly.

"Rosemary is a good, godly woman, and I'm happy that she's willing to leave her home and move here to be my wife. I want you to be happy with me."

Katy shook her head wildly. Her damp, loose hair flew across her shoulders and slapped her cheeks. "I can't be."

"Why?"

Dad's sad frown pierced Katy, but she hardened herself against it. "Because I don't want her. Because it's all happening too soon. Because ..." Katy ran out of reasons. Where were those debate skills when she needed them? *Katy 0- ...* She sank into her chair and put her head in her hands. Her hair spilled forward, giving her a shield. She didn't push it back.

Dad scooted his chair close and sat next to her. He put his arm around her shoulders. "Katy, I know this will be hard for you. It's been just you and me for a long time."

Katy nodded with her face still hidden behind her hair.

"But I want you to know that Rosemary is excited about having another daughter. With her own daughter so far away, she's missed her."

Oh, great. I get to be a replacement for her real daughter. Katy sniffed.

"And I think, once you get used to it, you'll be glad we asked Rosemary to become part of our family."

We didn't ask her—you did. "I think you're making a mistake, Dad." Slowly Katy raised her head. She pushed her hair over her shoulder and looked her dad in the eyes. "You're doing it again. You're bringing some lady from far away to Schellberg to be your wife. It didn't work for my mom—she didn't like it here. And now Mrs. Graber ... How do you know for sure she won't get tired of us and leave?"

Dad's lips formed a thin, grim line. "Your mother and Rosemary are two very different people."

"So you love Rose—Mrs. Graber more than you loved Mom?" Katy thought her chest might split in two while she waited for Dad to answer.

"That really isn't a fair question, Katy." Dad's voice sounded raspy.

"Why? Because it's true?" Katy couldn't believe her daring. The deacons would frown if they heard her speaking so rudely to an adult—especially to her own father. But the anger and hurt had to come out somehow.

"No, because it's impossible to measure love. Of course I cared for your mother or I wouldn't have married her. We had a child together, and a part of me will always be bound to her because she gave me you. But she's gone, Katy. She's been gone for a dozen years." Dad leaned back in his chair and ran his hand down his face. "It's time for both of us to move on. To quit thinking about Kate and open our hearts to someone else."

Katy lowered her head. She didn't want to open her heart to anyone else. No one would ever replace Kathleen Jost Lambright. Not as far as Katy was concerned.

"Now why don't you go on up to your room. Write in one of your new diaries, or take a nap. I'll call you when it's time to dress and go to Grampa and Gramma's."

Katy shifted her eyes to peek at her dad. "You mean you're going to do the dishes too?"

Dad laughed. Not a happy laugh, but more a nervous laugh. "Sure. I can do them. Go on up."

As Katy headed for the stairs, she thought, *Go ahead, Dad. Cook. Do dishes. Smile and be nice. But you can't win me over. That woman will never replace my mother.*

Chapter Sixteen

With her fork, Katy poked at the food on her plate. All of her favorites—roasted turkey with Gramma Ruthie's famous walnut and cranberry stuffing, mashed sweet potatoes swimming in butter and brown sugar, home-canned green beans, breaded tomato casserole, and fruited Jell-O salad—begged her to take up a bite and enjoy. But her rolling stomach refused to let her try so much as a morsel.

The entire family gathered around the huge trestle table in her grandparents' dining room, just like they had for as far back as Katy could remember. Grampa Ben and Gramma Ruthie sat at opposite ends. Katy and Dad across from each other. Aunt Rebecca, Uncle Albert, all of their kids from the twins down to three-year-old Trent, who was almost too big for the old wooden highchair, filled every spot. They sat so close their elbows bumped, but nobody complained. This was Christmas, and they were supposed to be together.

She glanced around at the smiling, happy faces. Even Aunt Rebecca looked cheerful today—her Christmas face,

Katy called it. Most of the time Aunt Rebecca looked as if she carried the weight of the world on her shoulders. Her relaxed, smiling face should have cheered Katy. But not even Aunt Rebecca's happy attitude could make a dent in Katy's armor of sadness.

After this Christmas, everything would change. Dad would be married. Maybe Mrs. Graber would want them to be with her family for Christmas instead of with Dad's. A lump grew in Katy's throat when she thought about Christmas away from Gramma Ruthie and Grampa Ben. Christmas wouldn't be Christmas without them!

Lola pointed to the basket of rolls that sat right in front of Katy's plate. "Katy, would you hand me the rolls, please?"

Katy automatically handed the basket to her cousin.

"Thanks." Lola plucked out a crusty roll and looked at Katy's plate. "What's wrong with you? You haven't even touched your food."

The question sounded like something Aunt Rebecca would say. Katy bristled. "I'm not hungry."

"Too bad. Everything is really good. And Mom brought chocolate lava cake for dessert. But you won't get any if you don't eat your dinner."

Katy shook her head. As if she were a six-year-old who needed to be threatened into eating! "I'm not hungry," she repeated, daring Lola with her eyes to challenge her again.

Lola shrugged and plopped the basket back on the table. "Then don't eat."

Even before everyone had emptied their plates, Aunt Rebecca scooted away from the table and scurried into the kitchen. An "oh!" of delight sounded when she returned with a huge, moist, dark chocolate cake on a platter.

Uncle Albert patted his stomach. "I'll take the first piece of that, Rebecca — and don't skimp on the size."

Aunt Rebecca clicked her teeth on her tongue, but her eyes sparkled. She sliced into the cake, and gooey pudding oozed from the center. Uncle Albert eagerly took a dessert plate, and Aunt Rebecca shot a smile around the table. "Who else is ready for dessert?"

Dad raised his hand.

"A big piece, Samuel?" Aunt Rebecca asked, knife poised.

Dad nodded. "Yes, but hold up for a minute. I have something to tell everyone."

He pushed back his chair and stood. He held his napkin in his hand, repeatedly squeezing the wad of linen.

Katy stared at his convulsing fingers and the twitching napkin. He was nervous. So was she. She held her breath.

Dad cleared his throat. "I guess all of you know the deacons gave their approval for me to court Rosemary Graber."

Everyone nodded. Katy bit down on the end of her tongue to keep from protesting.

"Well, Rosemary and I have talked, and ..." He gulped. His ears turned bright red. "She's agreed to become my wife. We plan to be married on the last Saturday in February."

Aunt Rebecca sucked in a huge breath. "Oh, Samuel ..."

"I'd say it's high time!" Uncle Albert socked the air with his fist and let out a whoop that scared little Trent into puckering up.

Gramma Ruthie clapped her hands, tears filling her eyes. "Praise be to God ..."

Grampa Ben rocked his chair and grinned. "Congratulations. We're so happy for you, son."

"Thanks, Dad. Thanks, everyone." Dad's shoulders rose and fell in a huge heave. "I can honestly say ... I've never been happier."

Katy swallowed hard. *Never been happier ... Never?*

The adults all jumped from their chairs and surrounded Dad, giving him hugs and patting his back. Lola and Lori leaned toward Katy, their faces wreathed in matching smiles. But Katy didn't smile back. She blinked rapidly to hold back tears. Her cousins' bright smiles faded into frowns.

"Katy, what's wrong?" Lori whispered, tugging at the purple sleeve of Katy's new dress.

Katy scooted away from the table. "Excuse me," she managed to choke out, then she dashed down the hallway to the bathroom. She closed herself inside and leaned against the door, her heart pounding. Seconds later, someone tapped on the door.

"Katy?" Lola's voice. "Can we come in?"

We ... That meant Lori was with her. Katy closed her eyes. The last thing she needed right now was a lecture from her cousins. Those two were becoming more like Aunt Rebecca every day.

"I—I'd rather be alone."

"Mom said we needed to check on you."

Katy sighed. If she didn't let them in, they'd go back and send Aunt Rebecca instead. Even though there were two of them, she'd rather deal with Lori and Lola than

Aunt Rebecca. She didn't have to be polite to the girls. With a grunt of irritation, she twisted the knob on the door and swung it open. "Just go tell her I'm okay."

The pair bustled into the bathroom. Lola closed the door then folded her arms over her chest. Lori adopted the same pose. Neither smiled.

Katy held her arms wide. "You can see I'm fine. You don't need to stay."

They exchanged a quick look. "You're not fine," Lori said, "and we know why."

Katy raised one eyebrow. "Oh?"

"Yes." Lola nodded hard, her cap ribbons bouncing. "You don't want a stepmother."

Sinking down to sit on the edge of the tub, Katy rolled her eyes. "Duh!" The word from the hallway at school left her throat before she had a chance to stop it. Her cousins gawked at her. "I mean," she said, drawing in a big breath, "who would?"

The twins scuttled forward and sat on either side of Katy on the rolled edge of the tub. Lola slipped her arm around Katy's shoulders. "I'm sorry, Katy. But you knew it had to happen sooner or later."

"Of course, it did," Lori added matter-of-factly. "Your dad's been alone a long time. Longer than any other widower in Schellberg. If it wasn't Mrs. Graber, it would be *somebody*."

Katy almost snorted. Did the twins actually think they were helping her?

"Be glad it isn't Mrs. Stoltzfus," Lori said.

"Oh, wouldn't that be awful?" Lola leaned forward and offered a horrified look. "She's fat and bossy, and her sons are as lazy as overfed hogs. You'd end up waiting on them hand and foot, just like the girl in that one story ... Oh, what was that, Lori?"

Lori tapped her lips. "Cinderella!" She shuddered. "Mrs. Graber is better than Mrs. Stoltzfus, that's for sure."

"Much better." Lola nodded emphatically.

"And just think, Katy," Lori went on, patting Katy's shoulder, "with another woman in the house, you won't have nearly as many chores. That will be a good thing, right?"

"Sure it will!" Lola answered as though Lori had asked her the question. "Even though Lori and I do all our house-cleaning, with two of us, it's never too much. Your life is going to get easier. You'll see."

Katy sighed. She appreciated that her cousins were try-ing to cheer her up. Usually, the two of them ganged up on her. Their behavior was a pleasant surprise. But they weren't exactly being realistic.

"Thanks, Lori and Lola. I'd like to think that you're right, but ..." Katy swallowed. "I don't think life will be easier. I'll have to answer to somebody new — somebody I don't even know. And she'll take over my house. It'll be-come *her* house. What if she brings her own furniture and stuff, and we have to take our stuff out? It won't even feel like home anymore ..."

Tears pricked her eyes, and she blinked several times to clear them. "And even worse, I probably won't see my dad anymore. He'll want to be with her instead of me. It's bad enough I have to compete with the stupid cows for his time, but when he gets a wife ..." She heard the selfish-ness in her tone, but she couldn't help herself. Everything she said was true. "Like you said, things are definitely going to change, but I don't think I'm going to like the changes."

She waited for her cousins to argue, to say, "You're wrong, Katy," or "You need to think about your dad, Katy," or even quote Bible verses. But for once they didn't. They sat silently, their heads low, their hands patting Katy's back in sympathy. In those moments, Katy liked them more than she ever had.

Suddenly, a knock at the door sounded. The three girls jumped. "Yes?" Lola called.

The door cracked open, and Gramma Ruthie peeked in. "What are you girls doing? We finished dessert, and we're ready to open packages. Are you coming out?"

The twins jumped up and dashed to the door. "We're coming!"

Katy rose more slowly. Gramma sent her a worried look. "Katy, are you feeling sick? You didn't eat your dinner, and now you're hiding in the bathroom."

"I'm fine," Katy said.

The look on Gramma's face indicated she didn't believe Katy.

"Honest, Gramma Ruthie," Katy insisted. She forced her lips into a smile. "I'm ready to open packages."

For a moment Gramma stood still with her lips parted, as if she was getting ready to say something. But she closed her mouth, offered a little nod, and held out her hand. Katy took it, just as she had when she was a little girl, and they walked down the hallway together. They reached the living room where everyone was sprawled on the furniture or the floor.

Dad looked up. A hesitant smile quivered on his lips. He patted the spot on the sofa next to him. A lump filled Katy's throat. She darted forward and slid into the spot beside her dad. But she couldn't relax.

Next year, the spot next to Dad would be filled by Mrs. Graber. Where would Katy belong then?

Chapter Seventeen

The last day of Christmas break sneaked up on Katy. She'd looked forward to two weeks of freedom—to sleeping late, writing long entries in her journal, and hanging out with Annika. But her break got filled with work: milking twice a day, helping Dad inject the cows with vitamins to stave off winter colds, helping in Aunt Rebecca's store ... Her break hadn't been hers at all. And it still hadn't snowed!

"What a lousy Christmas," she muttered as she dried the last of the breakfast dishes and put them in the cupboard. But Dad had promised to leave her alone today and let her do whatever she wanted.

She had her day all planned. First, she would write in her notebook journal. She hadn't opened one of the new ones Mrs. Graber had picked out, and she wasn't sure she ever would. Then she wanted to cut out the pieces for a new dress. After that, she planned to visit Annika and invite her for supper. Of course, that meant she'd have to cook a bigger meal, but it would be worth it to have some time with her friend. Other than the day they made candy, she'd had no time at all with Annika, and they still needed to exchange Christmas gifts. She hoped Annika would like the plaque she'd bought in town.

Katy whisked off her apron and hung it on the hook beside the back door. A movement outside caught her attention, and she pulled the curtain aside to peek. A familiar car pulled into the yard.

"Oh, great." She smacked the curtain into place. "The perfect way to ruin my last day of vacation — Caleb Penner!"

She whirled toward the stairs, intending to hide in her bedroom. A car door slammed, followed by a second one. Katy froze in place. Two car doors? That meant Caleb had brought someone with him. Curious, she crept back to the door and peeked outside again. Caleb and Annika were heading toward the house.

Katy flung the door open. "Come on in, Annika!" She flicked a look at Caleb. "Dad's in the milk room, washing out the tank."

Caleb grinned. "I'm not working this week, remember, Katydid?" He followed Annika through the door and clicked it shut behind him. He popped off his hat, leaving his hair standing on end. It reminded Katy of how Bryce's short-cropped hair stood up in the front like little spikes. She liked the way it looked on Bryce; on Caleb, it just looked uncombed. He must have noticed her staring at his hair, because he ran his hand over his head and smoothed the strands back into place. "I saw Annika in town, and she said she wanted to visit, so we both came." His smile grew, like he'd given Katy a gift by coming over.

Katy linked elbows with Annika and drew her into the kitchen. "I'm glad you're here. I was going to see if you wanted to eat supper with Dad and me tonight. We've hardly had any time alone my whole break." She hoped Caleb caught the hint and would leave now that he'd delivered Annika.

"I'd love to! I don't think Mom will mind," Annika said. She shot Caleb a questioning look. "Is that okay with you, Caleb?"

Caleb shrugged. "Sure."

Katy gawked at him. Since when was Caleb included in the invitation? She clenched her teeth.

Caleb added with a smirk, "I've eaten Katy's cooking before. It didn't kill me."

Annika hunched her shoulders and giggled, a shrill, girlish giggle she seemed to save for whenever Caleb was around. It grated on Katy's nerves. Annika gave Caleb's arm a playful smack. "Caleb, that's an awful thing to say! Katy's a terrific cook. But then, so am I . . ."

Katy rolled her eyes. If she had to watch Annika and Caleb flirt all morning, she'd lose her breakfast. Although she'd like to spend the extra time with Annika, it appeared she couldn't have Annika without Caleb. Looking straight at Annika, she said, "Well, plan on supper at six thirty. If you want to come a little early, we can do our Christmas gift trading before we eat."

Annika's face pursed into a pout. "You mean you don't want us to stay now? I hoped we'd have a whole day."

Katy sighed. Not if it meant Caleb would hang around too. "I have stuff I need to do," she said. "Sorry."

Once again, Annika shrugged. "Oh, well. I guess Caleb" — she scooted sideways a step and took hold of Caleb's skinny elbow — "can take me home then. I need to get your Christmas present anyway." She started guiding Caleb toward the door. "I'll check with Mom about tonight, but I'm sure it'll be okay. Should I come over around five o'clock?"

Katy sighed. "I'll be in the barn milking at five. Better make it six."

Caleb blurted, "I could come help your dad with the milking tonight. Then you girls would have more time together."

"Oh, Caleb, that's so nice of you!" Annika crooned. She turned eagerly to Katy. "Wouldn't that be better?"

"Dad gave you the week off," Katy reminded Caleb. Why was he so determined to weasel his way over here?

"I know but ..." Caleb rubbed his chin. His cheeks flushed pink. "You and Annika want time together. If you don't have to milk, you'll have more time. I don't have anything else to do, so ..."

"Let him, Katy," Annika prodded. She hugged Caleb's elbow to her side. "Consider it a Christmas present." She fluttered her eyelashes in Caleb's direction.

Katy didn't want a Christmas present from Caleb! And Annika's behavior was about to make her sick. "But—"

Caleb slipped away from Annika's hold. "I'll go ask Mr. Lambright and be right back." He darted out the door before Katy could stop him.

She glared at Annika. "Why did you bring *him* over here?"

Annika drew back, her face confused. "He already told you—he saw me in town, and I said I wanted to come out. So he drove me." Her voice turned defensive. "What's your problem?"

"*He's* my problem. This was supposed to be my break." *Partly a break from Caleb.* "You know how much he bugs me, always calling me Katydid and teasing me until I want to smack him." She altered her voice and mimicked his low, slow speech. *"I've eaten Katy's cooking before. It didn't kill me."* Balling her hands, she pressed them to her temple. "Ugh, I can't stand that guy! And then you act all sweet and gushy with him, and it makes me want to puke."

"Well!" Annika plunked her fists on her hips. "Pardon me for liking somebody without your approval. As if I *need* your approval." Annika tipped forward at the waist, her eyes snapping. "You know what your trouble is, Katy Lambright? You're jealous."

Katy dropped her jaw. "Jealous? Of what?"

"You're jealous of your dad because he's finally getting married and won't have to be alone anymore. You're jealous of me because I'm getting a boyfriend." Annika folded her arms over her chest and stuck her nose in the air. "You're jealous, and it's making you ugly."

"You think I'm jealous of you and Caleb?" Katy laughed. "As if! You're welcome to him! I don't give a — " Ugly expressions she'd heard at school quivered on her tongue. She swallowed them and finished, "a hoot about Caleb Penner! I think he's bubble-brained and unattractive to boot. You're welcome to him!"

"Ahem." The sound of someone clearing his throat came from the back door. Katy and Annika both jerked in that direction. Katy's face flooded with fire. Caleb stood in the doorway.

From the look on his face, Katy knew he'd heard every awful word she'd said. Even though she didn't like him, guilt hit her hard. She hadn't meant to hurt him. She held out one hand. "Caleb, I—"

He shook his head. "Don't worry about it." His eyes squinted half-shut, and his lips formed a firm, sullen line. "I just wanted to tell you your dad said it was fine for me to come milk tonight if you want time with Annika." He turned to head back outside.

Annika raced to his side and caught his arm "That is very sweet of you, Caleb, but it won't be necessary. I have no interest in spending my evening with Katy." She shot Katy a venomous look then turned a huge smile on Caleb. "Do you want to go to my house? We can play checkers or something, and you can eat lunch with us."

"Okay, sure." Caleb didn't sound very enthusiastic, but it didn't seem to bother Annika.

She beamed.

"Great! Let's go." She didn't even tell Katy good-bye as she hustled Caleb out the door.

Katy stood in the middle of the kitchen. Her throat ached, her nose stung, and she knew she was going to cry. Why was she losing everybody? She lost her mom to the world. She lost her dad to Mrs. Graber. And now she'd lost Annika to—of all people!—Caleb Penner.

"Why?" She asked the question out loud, almost like a prayer. But nobody answered.

At five o'clock Katy wandered out to the barn to help Dad with the milking. The cows stood in a restless line, eager to have their swollen milk sacs emptied. She quickly zipped into a pair of coveralls and entered the milking room. Dad turned from flipping the switch on his machine and gave Katy a surprised look.

"I thought Caleb was milking for you tonight." He hollered over the whir of the machine.

Katy shrugged and tried to look uncaring. "I told him not to bother. I can do it." A cow ambled into position. Katy deftly attached the suction cups and flipped on her milking machine.

Dad's eyebrows lowered, but the noise of the machine kept him from asking any questions. At supper, however, when Dad and Katy sat across the table from one another and dished up the chicken, broccoli, and rice casserole, Dad said, "I thought Annika was coming for supper."

A sting hit the back of Katy's nose. She sniffled. "She changed her mind." She scooped a bite of casserole into her mouth and focused on chewing.

"Oh?" Dad slathered a slice of bread with butter. "But weren't you girls going to spend the evening together? That's what Caleb said."

Katy put down her fork. "Dad ..."

Dad's hand paused midway to his mouth.

"Annika and I got into a fight."

"Oh?"

"Yes."

"So she decided not to come over?"

"Yes."

"Oh." Dad took a bite of the bread, chewed, and swallowed. "What was the fight about?"

Katy snatched up her fork and buried the tines in the casserole. "I don't wanna talk about it."

"Okay."

She and Dad ate in silence for a few minutes. Then Dad asked very quietly, "Was it about Caleb?"

Katy swallowed her bite without chewing and gawked at Dad. How could he have known? "Did you hear us?" Oh, she hoped he hadn't heard the awful things she'd said!

Dad chuckled. "No, I just guessed. We saw this coming."

The fine hairs on Katy's neck bristled. *We?*

"It's pretty obvious Annika likes Caleb." Dad cocked one eyebrow and gave Katy a quirky grin. "And it's just as obvious Caleb likes you. Rosemary said it was bound to cause problems, eventually."

Her again? That woman was infiltrating every fiber of Katy's existence! Katy pushed away from the table. Her chair legs screeched against the floor. Katy's voice mimicked the high-pitched sound. "Well, as usual, *Rosemary* was right. But he's a stupid boy. Annika is welcome to him. And I don't want you and Mrs. Graber talking about me!" She stormed for the stairs.

"Kathleen Lambright!" Dad rarely used her whole name. Doing it now let her know how angry he was.

Katy knew she'd been disrespectful. She knew she should go back. She knew she should apologize. Instead, she ran up the stairs, slammed herself in her room, and dove under the covers on her bed. She wished she could hide forever.

Chapter Eighteen

In the morning Katy looked at her reflection in the little mirror above the bathroom sink and groaned. All the crying she'd done the night before still showed in her puffy, red-rimmed eyes. If she had Jewel's makeup case, she could hide the evidence.

"But Mennonites don't wear makeup," she told her image.

With a sigh, she twisted her hair into a knot, tucked it under a cap, then hurried to her room to dress. Caleb and Dad were out in the barn milking, and Dad would be in soon for breakfast. She wouldn't make him wait, and she would prepare a big, hearty breakfast. Then she wouldn't have to verbally apologize. She hoped. She didn't think she'd be able to form the words.

As she set the table for breakfast, she remembered the look on Dad's face when she'd jumped up and yelled at him. Dad was a mild-mannered man, but he'd been mad. Really mad. She still wondered why he hadn't come charging up after her to demand an apology. Maybe he suspected the truth—that she wasn't sorry for what she'd said. She wished she hadn't screamed it at the top of her lungs, but she was glad she said it. He needed to know she didn't want Mrs. Graber's interference in her life.

She put several sausage links in a skillet on the stove and then stirred up a batch of waffle batter with cinnamon and raisins mixed in. Sweet scented steam rose from the waffle iron, mixing with the spicy aroma of sizzling sausage. Katy's stomach growled. She'd eaten little of her supper last night, and she was hungry. Dad would be too. Neither of them had cleaned up the supper mess, and leftovers were scattered all over the counter. Judging by amount of food left on his plate, he hadn't taken another bite after Katy left the table.

Guilt pricked again, but she pushed it down and refused to give it wing. He was in the wrong for bringing that woman into their lives. Pretending to be happy about it would be the same as lying. And now that she'd blurted out her real feelings, there was no need to pretend.

Dad came through the back door just as Katy removed the skillet from the stove. She pointed to the table where the waffles waited on a plate under an overturned serving bowl that kept them warm. "Breakfast is ready. I'll get the syrup."

"I'll eat later." Dad stood with his hand on the screen door's handle. "I just came to tell you I need to jump-start Caleb's car. Soon as I get him headed down the road, I'll take you to the bus stop. Eat without me." He stepped back outside.

Katy stood with the skillet in her hand and stared after him.

No smile.

No "Good morning, Katy-girl."

Dad never carried grudges ... until now. Regret wiggled through her, but she replaced the feeling with a dose of anger. *Fine! Let him stay mad!* She'd just stay mad too! She clanked the skillet onto the table, sat, and ate. The food that had smelled so good only minutes before tasted like sawdust, but she ate anyway. Then she stacked her dishes next to last night's supper dishes in the sink—they could just sit there all day and stink up the place!—and re-trieved her backpack. She could wait in the truck for Dad. And if he expected her to talk on the way, then he had another think coming.

When Katy got off the bus, she spotted Shelby, Jewel, and two other friends, Cora and Trisha, standing near the front doors of the school. A little smile tugged at her lips. The break had been awful—the worst Christmas she could re-member—but now she was back at school. A new semes-ter. A new start. A chance to have some fun. She hurried across the brown, crunchy grass to join the girls.

"Hi, Shelby! Jewel, Trisha, Cora ..." She greeted them by turn then looked around in curiosity. "Where's Bridget?" Katy secretly called Trisha, Cora, and Bridget the Three Musketeers after a book she'd read a few years ago. You never saw one without the other two.

Trisha made a face. "She's gone. Moved away."

Katy's mouth fell open. "Moved away? But when?" She flung an accusing look at the group. "Why didn't some-body tell me?"

Jewel snorted. "How could anyone tell you when you

don't have a phone? What were we supposed to use, Pony Express?"

Katy ducked her head so the others wouldn't see tears spring into her eyes. It wasn't fair! Bridget was one of her friends, and she hadn't even been able to tell her good-bye.

Cora sniffled. "She left yesterday. You knew her dad lost his job back after Thanksgiving."

Katy remembered Shelby telling her how worried Bridget had been. She'd promised to pray for the family, but she realized with a start she hadn't honored the promise. When everything started happening with Mrs. Graber, she'd forgotten all about praying for Bridget's dad. She'd let Bridget down.

Cora went on. "Her uncle in Arizona invited them to come stay with him and look for a job there. So they just packed up everything and moved."

"But so soon?" Katy could hardly believe how quickly things changed. Bridget here, part of their group, and then—boom!—gone. Just like that.

"People have to make a living," Jewel said in a way that made Katy feel stupid. "It's not like they had a choice."

"They had a choice," Katy argued, matching Jewel's tone. "There's always a choice. They could have kept looking for a job in Salina. They could have prayed and trusted God to take care of them. But they decided to move away without even saying good-bye."

"She *did* say good-bye," Jewel snapped back. "Just because you weren't around to hear it, don't take it out on us. Sheesh!" She stalked away with her back stiff.

Katy looked at Shelby. "Why's she so grouchy?"

Shelby's eyebrows rose. Katy expected her to ask why

Katy was so grouchy. Instead, she sighed. "Christmas wasn't all that great for her. Her mom was supposed to pick her up Christmas Eve and take her home for a day or two. Instead, her mom got picked up on a DUI, and the social services worker cancelled the visit. Jewel was really disappointed."

Katy understood disappointment. She'd had plenty of it herself this holiday. "What's a DUI?"

Cora giggled. "Katy, you're so funny. You don't know anything. DUI means driving under the influence. Jewel's mom was driving while she was drunk."

"Pretty stupid," Trisha added. "Jewel's better off without her mom."

"You'll never convince her of that," Shelby muttered.

Katy stared after Jewel, who paced back and forth beside some bushes. How many people were mad at Katy? Annika, Caleb, Dad, and now Jewel too. This year wasn't starting out so great. She sighed. "I better go talk to her." She started after Jewel, but the bell rang, and she turned around. She couldn't be late for class or then a teacher might be mad at her too. She would talk to Jewel at lunch.

In biology, the class watched a video on pond life. Katy tried to keep notes, as the teacher had instructed, but the uninteresting topic combined with dim lights and a narrator's droning voice nearly lulled her to sleep. Her eyelids felt heavy, and she bobbed her head so hard that her neck hurt. The class bell brought her fully awake, however, and she eagerly headed to her second-hour class.

She slipped into her familiar desk in the front row in the English classroom. Her classmates talked and laughed, more rowdy than usual. She supposed they weren't ready to give up their break from studies. But Mr. Gorsky quieted them with a raised hand and a stern look. As soon as they settled down though, he smiled.

"Welcome back, and happy new year." He pointed to the whiteboard behind him, where the word *neoteric* was printed in his bold, all-capped printing. "There's our word for the day." Then he chuckled. "Actually, that's going to be our word for the rest of the year."

One of the boys behind Katy called out, "Does that mean it's the last word for the year?"

"Oh, no." Mr. Gorsky shook his head, his mustache twitching. "Sorry, Keagan. We'll still have a new word each day. But this one is going to be our focus word for the semester."

Keagan groaned, but the sound faded into soft laughter.

Mr. Gorsky propped his hips against his desk and then folded his arms over his chest. "So who knows what *neoteric* means?"

Silence fell. Katy glanced around. The other kids appeared puzzled. No one seemed familiar with the word.

"Well then," Mr. Gorsky prompted, "somebody guess, based on the way it sounds."

The girl next to Katy raised her hand. "Does it have anything to do with hospitals and babies — stuff like that?"

A titter went around the room, but Mr. Gorsky swept it away. "I believe you're referring to *neonatal*, which isn't quite the same thing. But thanks for taking a shot at it. Anyone else?"

Keagan, the same boy who'd hoped it would be the last word, said, "I think I've seen *neoteric* before. Doesn't it have something to do with being smart?"

"Smart?" The boy next to Keagan snorted. "Yeah, right!"

"Actually," Mr. Gorsky said, "that's a step in the right direction."

Keagan punched his neighbor in the arm. "See there? I knew what I was talking about."

"I said it was a step in the right direction," Mr. Gorsky corrected. "I didn't say you'd found the destination."

Everyone laughed.

"Let's look at the first syllable by itself." The teacher pushed off from the desk and moved to the whiteboard. He picked up a blue marker and made a slash through the middle of the word. "Remembering that Keagan's guess is a step in the right direction, then what might *neo* mean?"

Katy crinkled her brow and stared at the shortened word. Then she wiggled her fingers.

Mr. Gorsky pointed at her with the marker. "Yes?"

"Does it have something to do with learning or thinking?"

"Yes!" Mr. Gorsky grinned. He turned and began slashing words onto the whiteboard as he spoke. "*Neoteric* is a fancy of way of saying someone is thinking in a way that hasn't been explored before. Used as an adjective, it means new or modern; as a noun, it refers to being a modern thinker. Being *neoteric* can be daring. Even radical. But basically it means thinking in new and different ways."

He dropped the marker into the tray at the bottom of the board and faced the class. "I want that word to be your challenge this semester. I want each of you to be forward thinkers—jumping outside the box instead of following what everyone else is doing."

Katy's scalp began to tingle. She liked the idea.

"We're going to continue studying classic literature." He waved his hands, stilling the complaining rumble. "But instead of studying it for the sake of plot, characterization, and motive, we're going to search for places where the author has made an attempt at *neoteric* thinking. And we're going to use *neoteric* thinking in our own writing." His flung his arms wide. "We're going to be bold! Daring!"

A few kids cheered.

"Because ..." Mr. Gorsky dropped the theatrics and sent the class a serious, teacher-ish look that brought everyone under control. "That's how new things—changes—happen. When someone is brave enough to step beyond what he's always done, a new world opens up. And new worlds are splendid places to explore."

No one said anything, apparently caught up in thought. Katy absorbed her teacher's words. For centuries, her ancestors had lived in the same way. In small, self-sufficient communities, abiding by a set of firmly set, well-ordered rules. Had the Mennonites ever considered being *neoteric*—modern thinkers? She felt fairly certain her dad and the deacons wouldn't approve of her exploring new ways of looking at old things. They would tell her she needed to remember that simplicity is best. To remember the unchanging Mennonite ways offered security and stability.

Secure and stable is good, she told herself, her muscles twitching with excitement, *for old folks. But I'm young. And I want to be neoteric, because new is fun and exciting.*

Chapter Nineteen

At the end of English class, Katy gathered her materials to leave. Mr. Gorsky stopped at her desk. He waved an envelope. "Kathleen, this came over Christmas break. It's from *Journalistic Pursuits*."

Katy's hands began to shake. She dropped her backpack onto the desk. "The magazine?" A few weeks ago, Mr. Gorsky had submitted her essay for possible publication in the periodical. This letter had to be their response.

"That's right. It's addressed to both of us, so I thought we should open it together."

Katy stared at the long, slender envelope. She nodded. "Yes, let's." A nervous giggle worked its way up her throat and escaped her lips. She quickly clapped her hand over her mouth.

Mr. Gorsky grinned. "Do you want me to open it?"

Without removing her hand from her mouth, she nodded vigorously.

He slid his thumb beneath the flap and pulled out a folded sheet of pale yellow paper. Katy lifted on tiptoe to glimpse a formal-looking letter with a fancy letterhead at the top. Mr. Gorsky held it out to her, but Katy was too nervous to read.

"Read it out loud," she said behind her hand, which had risen to cover her face.

Mr. Gorsky shook the paper, cleared his throat, and began to read. "'Dear Mr. Gorsky and Miss Lambright: Thank you for your submission to *Journalistic Pursuits*. As you know, this publication seeks to showcase the finest student works of literature in the country. The competition for placement in the magazine is stiff, and we are forced to decline many well-written pieces. Therefore, the authors of pieces that are accepted for inclusion should be congratulated. It truly is an accomplishment to be published in *Journalistic Pursuits*.'"

Katy frowned. Would they hurry up and get to the point?

"'It is with great pleasure,'" Mr. Gorsky continued, his voice rising in pitch, "'that we inform you that your essay, titled "A Recent Epiphany," has been chosen as the first-place essay and will appear in the May issue of *Journalistic Pursuits*. Congratulations to both teacher and student. Miss Lambright, we wish you much success in your future writing endeavors.'"

Mr. Gorsky slappped the letter with the backs of his fingers, making a loud *snap!* "Congratulations, Kathleen! I knew that essay was a winner!"

Katy cupped her cheeks with her hands and stared at him in shock. "*I* won ...? I really *won*?"

Mr. Gorsky laughed. "Well, of course you won. And you deserved it too. Your essay was very well-written. You should be proud of yourself." He folded the letter and slipped it back into the envelope. He put the envelope in her shaking hand. "I'm sure this won't be the last writing contest you win, either. You have a real gift, Kathleen. I hope you'll continue to use it."

Katy shook her head, the reality slowly sinking in. She'd won a writing contest. She would be *published* in a magazine. Joy filled her, making her feel as though she floated. *Oh, wouldn't Dad be proud!* Then her elation faltered. Dad was still so mad at her ... Would he even care when she told him?

Mrs. Graber would be impressed.

She gave herself an impatient shake. Who cared what Mrs. Graber thought? But Katy knew the woman would express pleasure. She'd picked out those diaries and the thesaurus for Katy's Christmas gifts. Whether Katy liked to admit it, Mrs. Graber would probably congratulate her more enthusiastically than many of her own family members.

The class buzzer rang, and students spilled into the English room. Katy jumped. "Oh! I'm late! I'm going to be in trouble."

Mr. Gorsky pointed her to his desk. "I'll write you a pass," he said, scribbling on a small piece of paper. He pressed it into her hand and offered another warm smile. "Congratulations again, Kathleen. I can't wait to see how you do in forensics. I have the feeling you're going to be one of our school's most proficient medal winners."

Katy held her good news inside until lunchtime, when she'd be able to tell all of her friends at one time. She couldn't stop smiling, though, which made Shelby shoot her curious glances during their final morning class. But each time Shelby asked what was up, Katy shook her head and mouthed the word, "Later." By noon Shelby's curious looks had taken on a hint of frustration, but Katy knew Shelby would understand when she finally heard the news.

Katy and Shelby joined Jewel, Cora, and Trisha at their usual spot in the cafeteria. Bridget's chair sat empty, giving Katy a jolt of sadness, but she pushed that feeling aside. She wanted to celebrate her winning essay. She quickly blessed her food, then she nudged Shelby with her elbow. "Guess what?"

Shelby put on a fakey scowl. "Oh, *now* you're ready to talk, when I want to eat this wonderful welcome-back-to-school lunch." She held up a bite of smothered steak that dripped running gravy. She sent a look around the table at the other girls. "Katy's harboring some secret. She's been grinning like the cat that swallowed the canary since she left English class."

Katy giggled, envisioning a smiling cat with a yellow feather stuck in its mouth.

Jewel took a swig of milk. "Well, don't keep us in suspense. What is it? We could probably use a little good news."

Cora and Trisha both nodded and prodded Katy to share.

Her shoulders hunched and lips pursed, Katy held out for a few more seconds to enjoy the anticipation. But when her friends' expressions began to transition from eager to irritated, she blurted out, "I won a writing contest. I'm going to be published in a magazine."

Jewel stabbed her fork into her green beans. "Oh, is that all? I thought it would be something really cool."

"Jewel!" Shelby reached across the table and popped

Jewel on the arm. Jewel yelped and jerked back, glaring at Shelby. Shelby ignored her. "That is totally awesome, Katy! Which magazine? When?"

Katy flicked a glance at Jewel before answering. *"Journalistic Pursuits."*

Trisha frowned. "I've never heard of that."

Cora said, "I have. Mr. Gorsky keeps a stack of them on the shelves in the back of the classroom. But I've never read one. They looked kind of boring."

Boring? How could anything with words in it be boring? Katy held the question inside. The last thing she wanted was for someone—most likely Jewel—to tell her she was weird. She explained, "They only publish student works, so it probably isn't really well known. But they said my essay won first place. It'll be published in May."

"An essay?" Jewel spoke around a bite of canned peaches. "Not a story?"

"No, but maybe I'll write a story next time." Katy's heart pattered at the idea of seeing a story she'd written appearing in a magazine—or maybe even a book someday!

"Well, it's pretty cool that they picked your essay," Cora said, but she didn't sound very enthusiastic. "I'll probably read it when it comes out."

"What's your essay about, Katy?" Trisha asked.

At least they sounded sort of interested now. Katy said, "It's called 'A Recent Epiphany,' and it talks about how I started school feeling like an outsider and like I didn't belong, but how I figured out I could belong and still be myself."

The girls stared at her as if she'd suddenly sprouted green feathers and a unicorn's horn.

"Oh," Trisha said.

"That sounds ... exciting," Cora added.

Jewel just kept eating.

But Shelby offered a bright smile. "I'm sure it'll be great, Katy. As soon as it comes out, be sure to tell us. We'll all read it. Won't we?"

"Oh, yeah. Sure."

Their lack of enthusiasm threw a bucket of cold water on Katy's joy. A lump filled the back of her throat—a sad lump. They began discussing their activities during Christmas break, and Katy turned her attention to eating. She had no desire to tell them what she'd done during break. *Wouldn't they all be so delighted to hear about my thrilling time in the barn milking cows and poking their thick hides with needles?* She'd written an essay—a winning essay—on how she'd found a way to fit in. But she hadn't. Not really.

The afternoon crept by as slowly as a snail across the ground. When time arrived to board the bus for the ride home, Katy could hardly wait to slink into a seat and block out the world. She leaned against her backpack, thinking about the letter inside. How she wanted to show it to Dad. To see happiness in his eyes. To hear him say, "That's wonderful, Katy-girl. I'm proud of you."

Tears pricked as she realized she wouldn't be able to show him the letter now. Not until this animosity between them ended. How could he be proud of her when he was so upset with her? Even though the bus heater roared, she shivered. She closed her eyes and tried to sleep, but the noisy students kept her from escaping into dreamland.

The driver pulled up at Katy's drop-off point. Dad's

pickup sat waiting, and she hurried off the bus. A suddenly frigid wind chased her across the dirt shoulder, and she climbed as quickly as possible into the warm truck cab. Dad shifted gears and took off without a word. The lump that had sat in the back of her throat since lunch grew, making it hard for her to breathe. Her heart begged her to say something—anything!—to end the silence between them, but her tongue refused to cooperate.

They reached the house, and Dad pulled in between the barn and the house like he always did. He shut off the engine, and Katy reached for the door handle. She couldn't wait to escape to her room and pour out her thoughts into her journal. If she didn't get there soon, she might explode.

But Dad stopped her with a single, low-toned word: "Katy."

She froze.

"I've made a decision."

Very slowly she turned her head and looked at him. He sat with his hands curled around the steering wheel and stared out the front window. She noticed he'd put her Christmas gift in the truck. The black cover looked shiny and out of place against the faded vinyl seat.

"You don't need to worry any more about Mrs. Graber. I went in to the market today and called her. I told her I changed my mind. I won't be getting married."

Surely, she'd heard him wrong. "W-what?"

"I won't be getting married." His lips hardly moved, and his voice was flat.

Katy squeaked out, "You won't? But ... but why?"

Finally, Dad shifted his head and looked at Katy. He

didn't look mad anymore. Just sad. And very, very tired. "You know why, Katy."

Yes, Katy knew. Because she didn't want Mrs. Graber as a stepmother. So Dad chose Katy over Mrs. Graber. It was exactly what she'd wanted. So why did that lump grow bigger instead of going away?

"Are ... are you sure?" She whispered the question, her tight throat raspy.

"I'm sure." Dad's face turned stern. "And we won't talk about it again. Now go on in and get supper going. The temperature's dropping, and the forecast calls for snow tonight. We might need to leave earlier in the morning to get you to the bus on time."

Snow. She'd longed for snow too. She slid out of the truck and headed for the house. What was wrong with her feet? Shouldn't she be skipping in happiness? A winning essay. No stepmother—she'd won! And snow on the way ... But her feet plodded instead of skipped. And Katy didn't know why.

Chapter Twenty

After she cleaned the kitchen, which took twice as long as usual since she had to wash the previous night's dishes as well as both breakfast and supper dishes from today, Katy headed to her room to do homework.

Since she didn't have biology homework, she pulled out her English notebook where she kept all the assigned words of the day, their definitions, and the sentences she created using them. She drew a curvy line beneath the word assigned the last school day of December and then penciled in her neatest handwriting, *neoteric*.

She pulled down her dictionary from the shelf above her desk and flipped it open to the N's. She carefully recorded the printed definitions, including the pronunciation guide and uses of the word both as a noun and as an adjective. It took awhile since she also recorded the word's origin, and the Greek words were tricky. Mr. Gorsky didn't require the origin to receive credit, but Katy wanted to remember all the different pieces of the words she learned. So she studiously recorded every bit of information from the dictionary.

That task done, she tapped her lips with the pencil eraser and considered sentences. She pressed the pencil to page and wrote: *I want to be a neoteric writer.* She wrinkled her nose. Too simplistic. She spun the pencil around and erased the sentence. After another few moments of thought, she recorded: *To be neoteric is to dare to be distinctive.* She let out a little snort. That sounded like a definition! She erased furiously, nearly rubbing a hole through the paper.

With her brows crunched into a fierce scowl, she closed her eyes and made herself think ... think ... think. And a sentence flew from her fingertips: *To be progressive, one must adopt neoteric aspirations; otherwise, life will remain stagnant and without the opportunity for growth.* A little long, but she liked it. And she couldn't help applying the thought to the lifestyle her parents, grandparents, and great-grandparents had chosen.

She couldn't imagine anyone thinking of the Mennonites as "neoteric" with their limited education and simple way of living. But then she sat upright with a thought. "Maybe the Mennonites aren't neoteric, but I am." She spoke aloud, wonder filling her frame. "I'm going to high school. I'm going to be published in a magazine. I might even go to college ..." *You'd make a very good teacher.* The words Mrs. Graber said the day they all ate at the Penners' house crept from her memory and rang through her mind.

She shook her head hard, sending thoughts of that woman away. "Dad isn't going to get married, so I don't need to think about Mrs. Graber anymore. But I *do* need to think about homework." Dutifully, she reached into her backpack for the rest of her books. But her hands stopped as a thought struck her.

If Dad didn't marry Mrs. Graber, she and Dad would stay the same. Just like the Mennonites, they wouldn't discover anything new.

Katy awakened early the next morning to a very cold room—colder than she could ever remember it being. Her nose, sticking out from beneath her covers, felt like ice. She wanted to pull the covers over her head and warm up, but she needed the bathroom. So, shivering, she wiggled out from under her blankets and snatched up her fuzzy robe.

As she left the bathroom, she encountered Dad on the landing. She hunched into her robe. "Why is it so cold in here?"

"I'm going down to check the furnace," Dad said. "It must have gone out." He wore his slippers and heavy plaid robe, the one that made him look like an old man. He hurried down the stairs, and Katy followed on his heels, hugging herself. She waited at the top of the cellar stairs, though. She hated the musty smell and creepiness of the dirt cellar. She only went down there if a tornado was coming.

"Is it out?" she called, bouncing from foot to foot to warm herself.

Dad came up, frowning. "It's out. And I can't get it to light for some reason." He stormed for the staircase leading to the second floor. Katy once again trotted after him. "I'll need to dress and go into town to see if Mr. Gebhart will come out to take a look at it." They reached the landing, and Dad paused outside his door. "If I'm not back in time, you'll have to help Caleb with the milking. Can you do that?

Of course I can do it. I've been doing it for years. She ignored his question and asked one of her own. "Does that mean I won't be going to school today?"

Dad grimaced. "Sorry, but that's a possibility if I'm not here. Unless you want to talk Caleb into taking you to meet the bus."

Katy didn't relish asking Caleb any favors, but maybe it would give her a chance to apologize to him. She knew she should do that, even if it would be hard to form the words. "I'll see what he says."

Dad closed his bedroom door behind him, so Katy darted into her room and dressed. She chose thick black tights instead of her usual anklets. She hated how the tights looked, but warmth had to come first today. She squirmed into a long-sleeved undershirt then pulled her dress over her head. Even with all the layers, the chill of the house went straight through to her bones. Before going downstairs, she put on her robe over her clothes. It would look silly, but it would help keep her warm. She hustled to the kitchen where she found Dad putting on his coat, scarf, and gloves.

"Use the stove to heat the kitchen," he instructed, "and go ahead and eat your breakfast. Leave something for me—I'll eat when I get back." He moved toward the door as he spoke. "Watch for Caleb and go out when he gets here—no sense in going out any earlier." He opened the back door. Bright light attacked, and Dad drew back. "Well, look at that ..."

Katy squinted against the sharp whiteness and scurried forward. The storm door window was completely covered in frost, so Dad cracked the door, and they both crunched one eye shut and peered out the narrow opening. Cold air whisked in, chilling her eyeball, but she couldn't stop staring. Her mouth fell open in an *O* of astonishment.

Snow! At least two feet deep in the yard, with drifts halfway up the barn on the north side. The front of the pickup truck looked buried beneath a thick meringue of white. Fluffy, glistening, Christmasy snow! But it came too late. How would she get to school?

Dad closed the door and looked at Katy with dismay on his face. "I don't think I'll be able to get the truck out in that, which means I can't go after Mr. Gebhart."

"What about school?" Katy asked. She hated missing class — catching up with the homework would be so hard.

Dad looked at her like she'd said something foolish. "Katy, if it snowed like that in Salina, they've probably cancelled school for the day. Go turn on the radio. Let's see if there are cancellation reports."

They kept their radio dial on the same station — a news station — and only used it to gather information. Static crackled the words, but after a few minutes of listening they discovered all the schools in Salina and its surrounding towns had been closed. Disappointment struck. Only one day back and this had to happen! Why couldn't it have snowed during Christmas break instead?

At least I won't have to catch up on a pile of homework, Katy consoled herself.

"Well, I doubt Caleb will be foolish enough to try to drive in this," Dad mused.

Katy didn't agree with Dad's assessment, but she knew Caleb's mother would be smart enough to keep her son home. "So I'll be your helper in the barn?" She smiled as she asked the question so Dad would know she wasn't complaining. It might actually be warmer out there with the heat from the animals.

"'Fraid so. But first, let's get some coffee going. We'll need it to warm us up."

While they sat at the table sipping the hot, strong coffee, Katy asked, "What if you can't get the furnace started, Dad? It's really cold in here."

"Jeff Reimer will get out his tractor, put on the big snowplow blade, and clear the roads, like he always does." Dad cupped his palms around his coffee mug. "It'll take him a while to get everything cleared, but surely by this evening, I'll be able to get into town for help."

"This evening? But—but—" Katy nearly yelped. Wouldn't they freeze to death by then?

"We'll keep the stove going," Dad said, "and just spend the day in the kitchen. If you get too cold, we'll bundle up and I'll walk you to the Gehrings'. They use woodburning stoves instead of a furnace, so they always have heat." A slight smile twitched at the corners of Dad's mouth. "It'll be a cold walk, but the wind's not blowing, so we can do it."

That meant being cooped up with Annika. As angry as Annika had been, Katy might find it colder at her friend's heated house than in her own unheated house. She said, "I should be okay here in the kitchen."

Dad added, "If for some reason Reimer doesn't get the road cleared and I can't get to town by supper, I'll want you to sleep at the Gehrings' tonight. It'll be too cold here for you after a day of no heat."

She put down her empty mug. "Okay. I'll get some breakfast started."

Katy spent most of the day sewing a dress. She brought the sewing machine into the kitchen and set it up on the table. The light wasn't nearly as good as the upstairs bedroom with its three big windows, but she had no desire to be in the chilly upstairs today. By three o'clock, Mr. Reimer hadn't shown up with his tractor plow, and Dad decided to take Katy to the Gehrings'.

"Bundle up good," he said. "Go ahead and put on some work coveralls, and tuck the legs into a pair of boots. We want to keep the snow off of you as much as possible."

Katy hated working in the barn in the ill-fitting coveralls — how would she walk for a whole mile in those things? But she didn't argue with Dad. Dad broke the path across the pasture for her, and following in his footsteps reminded her of when she was a little girl, always trailing behind him. He used to joke that he never stepped backward without looking because he knew he'd step on her.

The past weeks, fighting about Mrs. Graber, had robbed her of that close feeling with Dad. She wondered if she'd get the closeness back now that he had decided not to marry Rosemary Graber. She hoped so. She had missed him.

It took over an hour to walk the mile across the pasture to the Gehrings', and by the time they got there, Katy's feet felt frozen and her face was stiff from the cold. Dad pounded on the door, and Annika's mother answered. Her eyes widened in surprise when she spotted Dad and Katy on the rickety porch.

"Samuel and Katy Lambright! What are you two doing out in this blizzard?"

Katy stifled a giggle. A blizzard meant high winds and blowing snow. It might be cold and snowy, but it was calm. Apparently, Mrs. Gehring needed to check a dictionary.

Dad pushed Katy over the threshold. The warmth from the room greeted Katy, and her body shuddered in relief. Dad stomped his feet on the porch before stepping into the house. "Our furnace went out, so we don't have heat at our place, and I couldn't get to town to get help."

Mrs. Gehring shook her head, the black ribbons on her cap swaying. "Sometimes I think you men need to discuss having telephones at least in the barn so we can call for help when we need it. Do you two want to stay here?"

"I have to take care of the cows," Dad said, "but I'd like it if Katy could stay the night. It's just too cold at our place."

"Of course she can!" By Mrs. Gehring's warm welcome, Katy knew Annika hadn't told her mother about their disagreement. Mrs. Gehring patted Katy's shoulder. "She's welcome to stay as long as she needs to. She'll just bundle in with Annika, like they used to when they were little." She turned toward the back of the house and bellowed, "Annika!" Facing Katy again, she smiled. "She's mixing dough for cinnamon rolls for tomorrow's breakfast. Does that sound good?"

Annika scurried into the room. "What is it, Mom?" Her curious expression turned stony when she saw Katy, and she clamped her mouth shut.

"Katy's spending the night — no heat at her house," Mrs. Gehring explained briefly. "Take her on up to your room so she can get out of those wet coveralls. She might need to put on one of your dresses if her clothes underneath are wet too." She turned back to Dad. "Don't you worry, Samuel. We'll take good care of Katy. Do you want to stay for a while and warm up? Dale has all the stoves roaring. We've been just fine today." She almost looked smug.

Dad shook his head. "I better head back — milking time soon." He offered Katy a smile. "'Bye. Stay warm."

"'Bye, Dad," Katy said and watched him head back onto the porch.

Mrs. Gehring closed the door with a snap then swished her palms together. "Annika, are you still standing there? Do what I said before Katy catches a cold."

"Yes, Mom. C'mon, Katy." But even though Annika moved in obedience, Katy knew that inwardly she was rebelling.

Chapter Twenty-One

Annika opened her wardrobe and yanked out a dress. She tossed it onto the bed and said in a flat voice, "There. Use it if you need it." She whirled and headed for the bedroom door.

Katy scuttled forward and caught Annika's arm. If they were going to spend the night together, she intended to clear the air now. She wouldn't spend hours tiptoeing around Annika and pretending everything was okay when they were in front of her family then sit in chilly silence when they were alone. "Wait."

Annika shrugged loose. "What? You've got a dry dress. Change. I've got work to do."

Katy let out a huff. "Annika, just stop it! The dough can wait for a minute or two. Will you listen to me?"

Folding her arms over her chest, Annika glared at Katy. Obviously, she wasn't going to make this easy.

Katy looked directly into Annika's angry face and said softly, "Will you let me apologize for yelling at you the other day? I wasn't mad at you, but I took it out on you, and I shouldn't have. I really am sorry."

Annika's expression didn't soften. "You hurt my feelings. And you hurt Caleb's feelings. What you said wasn't nice at all."

Katy ducked her head. "I know." Even though she'd spoken the truth, she knew it was better to be kind than to blurt everything she thought, true or not. "I feel bad that Caleb heard me. And I plan to apologize to him the next time I see him." She looked at Annika again. "And in a way, you were right."

Annika's brows came together. "About what?"

"About me being jealous."

A slight smirk formed on Annika's lips. "I thought so."

"But not of you and Caleb," Katy quickly clarified. "Of my dad and Mrs. Graber. I didn't like that Dad spent so much time with her. I felt like she was replacing me, and it made me mad. But honestly, I don't have any interest in Caleb for a boyfriend. You can have him."

Annika rolled her eyes. "He isn't yours to give." The words were snotty, but her tone was mild. She was losing her anger.

Katy said, "I know. I just meant I'm not going to compete with you for him. If you want him for a boyfriend, that's fine, and I'm not jealous at all." *There's somebody else I like.* She hadn't seen Bryce at school at all yesterday. And she wouldn't see him again until all this snow cleared. The thought made her lonely for him.

"Well, I suppose that's good to know." Annika picked at a loose thread on her sleeve. "But you're going to have to get over your jealousy for Mrs. Graber. Once she marries your dad, she'll be around all the time, and you'll be miserable if you don't learn to accept her."

Katy didn't much like being lectured by Annika. Besides, Annika didn't know everything. For once, Katy knew something before anybody else. She smiled. "Oh, it's not a problem anymore. She isn't marrying my dad."

Annika's chin jerked up, and she met Katy's gaze. "What?"

Her surprised reaction was very satisfying. "My dad changed his mind. He isn't going to get married after all."

Annika shook her head slowly back and forth with her eyes wide. "Oh, Katy, that's terrible."

Katy jolted. Terrible? "Why?"

"Your dad was so happy ..." Tears actually appeared in the corners of Annika's eyes. "Everyone said so. And everybody thought Mrs. Graber was perfect for him." She wiped her eyes. "Why'd he change his mind?"

Guilt sat like a rock in Katy's gut. She pressed her palms to her stomach. "I—I'm not really sure." *Liar!* The rock grew, making her feel queasy.

Annika sighed. "Well, I suppose it's for the best, but even so ..." She shrugged. "I hope he finds someone else to marry then. I'd hate to see him spend the rest of his life alone." Suddenly, she gave a little jerk, like someone poked her. "Oh, my cinnamon rolls! I need to get to the kitchen. Change your clothes, Katy, then you can come down and help me." She ran out the door.

Katy sat on the edge of the bed and began to tug off her boots. Annika's comment hung in the room, stinging Katy's senses the same way smoke from a fire stung a person's nose. *I'd hate to see him spend the rest of his life alone.* In less than three years, Katy would finish high school. After that, she hoped to get permission to go to college. If she left for college, then Dad would be the only one in the house. The image of Dad all alone in the house pierced Katy's heart and made her nose sting even more.

Annika said everyone had noticed changes in Dad. Katy had seen them too. He'd seemed less tired and stressed. He'd laughed more and talked more. She'd liked the re- laxed Dad — she just hadn't liked that it was Mrs. Graber making the changes. The rock in her stomach began to roll around as she thought about Dad becoming sad and quiet again.

She still didn't like the idea of Dad marrying Mrs. Graber. She didn't like the idea of Dad marrying *anyone*. But was it fair that he should give up his chance for a wife just to please Katy? He'd even said he didn't look forward to being alone when she was old enough to leave home.

With a groan, Katy covered her face with her hands. Tears pricked behind her closed lids. *What's the right thing to do?* The question squeezed from her aching heart. She looked toward the ceiling and asked it again: "God, what is the right thing to do?"

Neoteric ... The word from English class seemed to bop her on the nose. How could *neoteric* be the answer? But things started falling into place, like pieces of a puzzle. Every fairy tale she'd read depicted the stepmother as a bad person who didn't care for her stepchildren. Marlys had worked to get rid of her stepparents because she didn't want them in her life. Katy was acting just like them by rejecting Mrs. Graber. She wasn't being modern in her thinking at all.

And was it fair? Tears threatened again as she thought about Mrs. Graber complimenting her, choosing Christmas gifts for her, sewing her a dress out of fabric that Katy loved. Yes, the woman had taken Dad's attention, but she'd also tried to give Katy attention. And Katy had pushed it away.

She whispered, "I know what I need to do." But could she be brave enough — and unselfish enough — to do it?

By the next morning, Mr. Reimer had made the rounds with his tractor, and Dad was able to drive to the Gehrings' and retrieve Katy. Katy gave Annika a hug at the door and whispered, "Thanks for letting me come over. I had fun." She and Annika had stayed awake talking and giggling into the early morning hours. She was so glad they were friends again.

When Katy got in the pickup, Dad said, "I'll run you home so you can change. It's too late for the bus, but I'll drive you into school so you won't miss the whole day."

"Oh, thanks, Dad!"

"You're welcome. I know you enjoy your classes."

Dad drove slowly over the hard-packed snow, and Katy stared out the frosty window across the white landscape. Already the sun was beginning to melt the drifts. Even though the snow had come too late for Christmas, it made her a little sad to think of it melting away so quickly. The way Dad's happy countenance had melted away after he'd told Mrs. Graber he wouldn't marry her.

Katy spun to face Dad. "Dad, can I talk to you about something?"

Dad kept his eyes on the road and nodded.

"It's about Mrs. Graber."

Dad sent her a frowning look. "I thought I said we weren't going to talk about her anymore."

"I know what you said, but I need to. Okay?"

For several seconds, Dad didn't move or speak. But finally he nodded.

Katy drew in a deep breath. "I shouldn't have interfered in your relationship with Mrs. Graber. If ..." She gulped, praying for the strength to get the words out. "If she makes you happy, then I want you to marry her."

Dad grabbed the gearshift and jerked it while applying the brakes. The truck came to a shuddering halt. Dad set the brake then angled himself to stare at Katy. "What did you say?"

She couldn't tell if he was mad or shocked. A nervous giggle tried to escape, but she managed to swallow it. "I want you to marry her."

Dad tipped his head. "Why?"

"Because ... because she makes you happy. And I want you to be happy." Tears flooded Katy's eyes and spilled down her cheeks. Before she could stop herself, she began to sob. "I'm sorry, Dad! I was mean and selfish and jealous. I thought if you married her then you'd stop paying attention to me. It was stupid. But you really like her, and I know you were happy when she was around, and I just don't want you to go back to being sad again, and I don't want you to be mad at me forever. So call her back and tell her you want to marry her, okay?"

He sat in stunned silence.

She grabbed his arm. "Okay, Dad?"

Dad pulled her into an awkward hug. She buried her face against his chest and continued to cry. She wished she could stop. She felt like an idiotic baby. But somehow it also felt good to release all of the pent-up emotions of the past few days.

Dad rubbed her back for a couple of minutes then set her aside. He pulled a blue handkerchief from his pocket. "Here. Clean up your face. You're a mess." He smiled as he said it.

Katy wiped her eyes and blew her nose. She sat holding the handkerchief in her lap. She'd said her piece. Now it was up to Dad.

Dad pinched his chin between his finger and thumb for a few minutes, as if he was gathering his thoughts. Finally, he looked at her and spoke softly. "Katy, I don't want you to think that I can't be happy without a wife. If I led you to believe that I wasn't happy before Gramma brought Rosemary to Schellberg, then I've done something wrong. I've had a good life. I have a daughter I love very much. I've been happy."

"But you smiled more when she was around," Katy pointed out.

Dad grimaced. "Maybe I did. God created us to be social beings. It's natural for me to want a wife, just as it's natural for you to think about marrying and having a family someday."

Katy ducked her head, her ears heating up as she considered being courted.

Dad went on. "I admit I enjoyed having an adult to talk to and share things with. I tend to worry too much about things, and Rosemary helped me relax. But that doesn't mean I can't be happy without her. Do you understand that?"

Katy nodded slowly. "I think so. But you got so mad at me when I didn't act like I liked her ..."

"I never want to see you be disrespectful to any adult." Dad's tone turned a bit stern, but then it softened. "But I shouldn't force my views on you, either. I was wrong to try to *make* you like her."

"So will you call her?"

Dad sighed. "I don't know, Katy-girl. I appreciate your apology — it means a lot to me that you're willing to accept her. But when I called her the other day ..." He shook his head. "I hurt her. A lot. I don't know what she'd say if I called and told her I'd changed my mind again. I don't know if she'd trust me."

Katy grabbed Dad's hand. "But you have to try, Dad! You have to be neoteric sometimes."

Dad's brows made a V. "Huh?"

"New in your thinking. Taking chances," she babbled. "You won't gain anything if you don't try, right? Just like me asking to go to school. I knew you and the deacons might say no because no one had ever done it before, but I still had to try because it meant so much. If ..." She gulped. "If Mrs. Graber means that much to you, then you have to try. W-will you try, Dad?"

He nibbled his lower lip and stared out the window for a long time. Then he put the truck in gear and the wheels crunched on the snow as the truck rolled forward. Finally, he said, "I'll think about it."

Katy sat back in the seat. She couldn't ask for more than that.

Chapter Twenty-Two

Dad walked Katy into the school office so she would be excused for being late. The secretary gave her a pass for her third-hour class. "But it's almost over," the woman said, "so you might not make it in time. If not, throw the pass away and go on to lunch."

Katy thanked the secretary, told Dad good-bye, and headed down the hall. Her head low and feet moving fast, she didn't realize anyone was stepping into her pathway until she slammed into him. She bounced back and covered her mouth with her hand. "Oops!"

Bryce Porter waved his arms and rocked on his feet like he was about to fall. Just when Katy was ready to grab his arm and steady him, he smiled and made a little bow. "Well, Katy Lambright, how nice to run into you."

She giggled. With his close-cropped hair, tucked in button-up shirt, and khaki pants, he could almost pass for a Mennonite youth. Except for those little spikes of red-blond hair standing up in the front. The Mennonite boys always combed their hair flat. "I'm sorry," she gasped. "I should've been watching where I was going."

He shrugged. "No harm done." He reached out, plucked the pass from her hand, and read it. "Ah ..." He gave it back. "How come you were late?"

"Too much snow — we couldn't get out," she replied. She knew she should hurry on before the bell rang, but she enjoyed talking to Bryce. He made her feel ... real.

"Didn't the road crew clear your roads for you?"

She shook her head. "The county crew doesn't come out to Schellberg. One of the men from our fellowship uses his tractor and snowblade to do it for us. But it takes a while."

Bryce nodded. "Oh, cool. Nice to have someone around to handle it for you folks."

He didn't act like he thought it was weird that a Mennonite man driving a tractor took care of the snow, but Katy wasn't sure what he meant by "you folks." She didn't want to think Bryce saw her as set apart from the kids at school. Especially not from him.

She waved her hand toward the classroom door. "I better hurry before the bell rings." She inched her way down the hall.

"Oh, yeah ..." Bryce started walking backward in the opposite direction. "I was heading to the office to grab some papers for Ms. Ingler, and she's waiting for them. See you later, Katy." He turned his back.

She stared after him. Did he sound disappointed to stop talking to her? She hoped so.

Suddenly, he whirled around and faced her. "Hey!"

"What?" Her ears went hot at being caught watching him.

"You're going out for forensics, right?"

She nodded.

"It starts after school today."

She nodded again. She'd had it on her calendar for a couple of weeks already.

"So I'll see you then, right?"

Katy swallowed. He looked so hopeful it made her heart gallop. "Y-yes. I'll see you then."

"Cool. 'Bye, Katy."

She reached the classroom door just as the bell rang. She wiggled her way past the stream of leaving students to give the pass to her teacher, then she turned around and followed the others. She caught up with Shelby and walked with her to the lockers.

"What did you do on your snow day?" Katy asked.

"Slept all day!" Shelby laughed. "How about you?"

Katy dropped her backpack in her locker and waited for Shelby to do the same. Then they turned toward the cafeteria. "Mostly shivered."

"What?"

Katy laughed at Shelby's expression. Then she explained the day without heat. Somehow talking about her frosty nose and having to stay in the kitchen all day seemed funny, and she and Shelby giggled as they went through the line. Jewel, Trisha, and Cora were already sitting at their table, waiting. They looked up when Katy and Shelby approached.

"What's so funny?" Cora asked.

"Katy is," Shelby replied. She plopped her tray onto the table and slid into a chair. "Tell 'em about your day yesterday, Katy."

Katy sat down and folded her hands to pray. Then she raised her head and opened her mouth to tell the others about her heatless day. But before she could say anything, she spotted Bryce walking toward their table. She sat with her mouth open until he reached the table. Then she closed her mouth so suddenly her teeth clacked. What must he have thought of her sitting there with her jaw hanging slack?

But he didn't act like anything was wrong. He grinned. "Hey, Katy, I just *ran into*—" He winked, and Katy thought she might melt through her chair. She knew what that wink referred to! "—Mr. Gorsky, and he asked if you still had that letter from *Journalistic Pursuits*."

Katy nodded. She intended to paste it in her scrapbook.

"Could you maybe bring it to school tomorrow? He forgot to make a copy of it, and he'd like to have it for his records."

"Yes. Sure. I'll do that." Why did her voice sound all squeaky? And why was she breathing so hard? Must be all the laughing she and Shelby had done. *Yeah, right.*

"Oh! And about forensics . . . You were gonna do original oration, right?"

Not trusting her voice, she simply nodded.

"Great. Do you know what you'll write about?"

Oh, yes. Over the past few days, Katy had decided on a perfect topic. One she knew she could address with passion. "Uh-huh," she gulped.

Bryce flashed a bright smile. "Figured you'd be ready to go. Can't wait to hear it for the first time. Bet you'll knock the judges' socks off." He took a backward step, his eyes never drifting from hers. "See you after school in forensics, Katy." He spun on his heel and strode toward the end of the lunch line.

Katy stared after him. He paused to high-five a friend.

Then a few steps further he bent forward to whisper something to someone and then laughed. Bryce was so cute, so confident, so easygoing. And he chose to talk to her.

"Earth to Katy."

Katy jumped. She looked at Jewel, who sat smirking. Trisha and Cora snickered.

"Looks like our Katy has a crush," Jewel said.

Katy's ears flamed so hot she feared smoke would rise.

Shelby nudged Jewel's tray with her own. "Aw, c'mon guys, don't make fun." She grinned. "I think it's kinda cute that Bryce likes Katy. And if she likes him back, then ..."

Katy jerked her head toward Shelby so fast the ribbons from her cap flew in the air. "You think he likes me?"

Shelby gawked at Katy. "Duh!" She laughed, and the other three girls joined in. Then Shelby sobered. "That won't get you in trouble, will it? I mean, if you like someone who isn't Mennonite?"

Oh yes, it could definitely cause trouble ... But it wasn't as if Bryce had asked to court her the way Annika hoped Caleb would ask to come courting. And how would anyone in Schellberg even find out? Nobody else attended this school. They'd only know if Katy told.

Suddenly, she felt sneaky again, and she didn't like it. She said, "It doesn't matter because Bryce and I are just in forensics together. We're not even really ... friends." The admission made her sad.

Jewel shrugged. "Well, too bad. He's kinda cute, in a geeky sort of way. And he goes to the Bible study group all the time. I even see him pray before he eats. He'd probably be perfect for you, Katy."

No he wouldn't, because he isn't Mennonite.

By forensics time, the muscles in Katy's neck were as tight as knots in a wet rope. She tried to stay focused on Mr. Gorsky's instructions and avoid looking at Bryce. She didn't want to give him ideas. Yet she couldn't stop sneaking glances at him. When she didn't catch him looking back, she felt like crying. *You're acting like a ninny,* she told herself, but it didn't matter. Jewel was right; Katy had a crush. And even though she shouldn't even be *thinking* about Bryce, she couldn't seem to help herself.

Mr. Gorsky handed out packets of information about the categories for competition. She strained to see which packet Bryce took and caught the word "duet." Duet meant two, so whatever he was doing, it was with someone. But who? She looked around the room at the other students. She hoped Bryce wouldn't pair up with Marlys or one of the other really popular girls. How could she possibly compete with the pretty girls, with their stylish clothes and airs of confidence?

Katy, knock it off! She needed to stop worrying about Bryce and his partner and think about her own category. Mr. Gorsky expected her to win medals. She couldn't win medals if she was thinking about Bryce instead of the competitions. She hunched over her desk and began reading the expectations for a person competing in the original oration category. A shrill giggle interrupted her focus. She glanced over her shoulder. Disappointment hit as hard as if a piece of the ceiling had fallen on her head.

Bryce had his head close together with Marlys, and they were laughing together.

+

When the bus pulled up to Katy's stop, she noticed Grampa Ben's car waiting instead of Dad's truck. She climbed in, greeted her grandpa with a kiss on his cheek, then asked, "Where's Dad?"

Grampa grinned. "In town. At the market."

Katy's heart leaped into her chest. "Is he . . . shopping?"

Grampa put the car in gear and laughed. "Oh yeah, but not for food."

And Katy knew what Dad was doing—following her advice. She'd told Dad to try to reconcile with Mrs. Graber, but a part of her still worried about all the changes that would come into her life if she gained a stepmother. Two different hopes battled for prominence in her heart. On the one hand, she hoped Mrs. Graber would say yes for Dad's sake—but on the other hand, she hoped Mrs. Graber would say no so Katy wouldn't have to worry about changes.

Neoteric . . . no change, no opportunity to explore something new. The sentence she'd constructed for her assignment came back to haunt her. She closed her eyes and winged a quick, silent prayer to heaven: *God, let whatever is best for Dad, me, and Mrs. Graber happen.* It helped her to give God responsibility for solving the problem. But a little bit of her still worried.

"I'm s'posed to take you into town to meet him," Grampa was saying. "There's a good sale on canned goods, and your dad didn't know what you had left in the cupboards. He wants you to stock up."

As if she could think about canned goods at a time like this! But she said, "Sure, Grampa."

When they reached the store, Katy saw Dad standing inside the main door. She thanked Grampa for the ride and dashed inside the market. She gasped out, "What did she say?"

Dad didn't smile, but he didn't frown either. He raised one shoulder in a shrug. "She's going to think about it and pray about it."

"What if—what if she decides not to marry you?" Katy thought she'd be able to understand how Dad would feel if Mrs. Graber chose to reject Dad. Her heart still stung from seeing Bryce and Marlys so friendly with each other.

A very small smile quivered on the corners of Dad's lips. "I'm planning to be in prayer too, Katy-girl. Rosemary and I want God's will first, for us and for you."

Katy nodded slowly. Maybe she should be praying for God's will concerning her friendship with Bryce instead of worrying about it.

Dad slung his arm around her shoulders. "Now c'mon, let's get this shopping done so we can head home."

"Okay, but ..." Her mind raced. She wanted to do something but didn't want Dad to know about it. Not a sneaky thing—a good thing. She pulled a squeaky rolling cart from the line and pushed it toward Dad. "Could you maybe get started picking out cereal and bread? I need to ..." She waved her hand in the direction of the back of the store.

Dad grinned. "Sure, Katy, go ahead. I'll wait for you in the cereal aisle."

"Thanks." She escaped. She felt a little guilty; she'd led Dad to believe she was going to the bathroom. But she couldn't tell him what she really wanted to do. He might think she was interfering again.

She darted into the little cubby where the town's telephone hung on the wall. On a little shelf below the telephone, Katy spotted the notebook where people recorded the calls they made so they could come in and pay when the bill arrived. She had no trouble locating Dad's name and the number. Mrs. Graber's number. She didn't know whether it would connect directly to Mrs. Graber — were the Mennonites in Meschke allowed to have their own phones? — or a public place, but she'd either deliver her message directly to the woman or leave it for her.

Resting the handset in the cradle of her neck, she underlined the number Dad had dialed with one finger and used her other hand to dial. A blaring ring carried through the line, and Katy squared her shoulders. She'd apologized to Dad. Now she needed to apologize to Mrs. Graber and let her know she had Katy's blessing to become Mrs. Samuel Lambright.

Chapter Twenty-Three

On Friday morning, Katy's alarm clock rang a half hour earlier than usual so she could have a little extra time. She intended to go out to the barn and talk to Caleb when he arrived to help with the milking. Dad had given her a funny look when she'd told him at supper the night before that she needed to talk to Caleb in private, but he hadn't questioned her. She was glad. It would be hard enough to apologize to Caleb. She didn't want to have to tell Dad how awful she'd been.

As soon as Caleb's car pulled into the lane, she dashed outside. She met him as he slipped out of the driver's seat. "I need to talk to you," she blurted, and his freckles faded under a blaze of pink. She ignored the blush and pointed to the barn. "In there. It's cold out here."

He followed her to the barn, breathing so hard little clouds hovered on her shoulder. They stepped inside the big structure, and Katy whirled around to face him. She'd rehearsed the apology so many times in her mind last night that it tumbled out in a rush.

"I'm sorry about what I said to Annika. It was rude and

hurtful, and I should have kept it to myself. I know I hurt your feelings, and I'd like to ask you to forgive me."

He stood with his mouth slightly open, staring at her for a long time. Then a little grunt sounded. "So you meant it?"

She blinked and took a step backward. "What?"

"What you said that day . . . You just told me what you said was rude . . . and hurtful . . . and you shouldn't have said it." He flicked his fingers in the air one by one, counting off her remarks. "But you didn't say you didn't mean it. So you really think I'm stupid and ugly?" He didn't repeat her exact words, but he remembered the meaning.

Heat grew in her ears, all the more intense because of the cooler temperature of the barn. She gulped.

He shrugged. "It's okay, Katydid. I know I wasn't the smartest kid in school, and I know I'm not good-looking. You didn't say anything I didn't already know."

The burning in her ears increased. Even though he tried to act like it didn't bother him, she could see by the look in his eyes he was still hurt by her words. Katy threw away the practiced speech and shared honestly with Caleb. "Do you know why I said those things?"

His gaze flicked to the side. He scuffed his toe in the dirt. "Not really. I guess you were mad?"

She nodded and yanked on his arm so he'd look at her. "Yes, I was mad to see you coming. Because you tease me and say things that irritate me."

Streaks of red colored his freckled cheeks.

"You call me Katydid even though I've told you over and over I don't like it. You made fun of my cooking." Katy kept an even tone so Caleb would know she wasn't mad now. "You stick your nose in when I'm talking to Annika instead of giving us privacy. Caleb, sometimes you just aren't polite, and it bugs me."

He sniffed and seemed to examine the barn rafters.

"But even so," Katy continued, "I was wrong to say what I did. No matter how angry I am, I shouldn't be deliberately hurtful, and I was that day. I am sorry, Caleb. Will you please forgive me?"

"Sure, Katy." His reply came so fast it seemed like his tongue tripped over his teeth. "I better get to work now." He darted around her and shot into the milk room.

Katy sighed and headed back to the house. She met Dad halfway across the yard.

"Did you get things settled with Caleb?"

She nodded. She'd said her piece. Now it was up to Caleb to keep pestering her or stop it.

"So is he going to ask if he can court you?"

"Dad!"

Dad laughed and held up both hands. "Okay, okay!"

Then Katy thought of something else. "Speaking of courting ... have you heard from Mrs. Graber?"

Dad's laughter died. He said, "I'm supposed to go to the market tonight at seven o'clock. She'll call then."

"So you'll know tonight?"

"I'll know tonight."

Katy drew in a big breath. "Tonight ..." *Neoteric* — new, or same-old, same-old? She'd know by bedtime.

Dad jerked his chin toward the house. "Go eat your breakfast now and get those dishes out of the way. We'll leave for the bus soon."

❖

Katy thought the day would never end. Although she needed to pay attention in class, her thoughts kept drifting to Meschke and Mrs. Graber. What would she say to Dad tonight? When she'd talked to the woman, she'd been very kind. She'd thanked Katy for apologizing and assured Katy she understood why she had reservations. They'd had a nice, air-clearing chat, but she hadn't given Katy any clues as to whether she'd marry Dad.

If she said no, how would Dad react? If she said yes, would Katy be able to accept it? Again and again she looked at the clock on the wall, willing the hands to go faster so the evening would come and all the worrying and wondering would be over.

At home, she fixed a simple supper of omelets and toast. It wouldn't have mattered what she fixed—neither she nor Dad ate much. Katy kept searching Dad's face, hoping for clues for what he was thinking. But if he was scared or nervous, it didn't show. If he hadn't kept glancing at his wristwatch instead of eating, she might have thought it was a normal evening on the dairy farm.

At quarter to seven, Dad put on his billed cap and coat. "Well, this is it," he said.

Should she say "good luck"? Uncertain, Katy just nodded at him.

His chest expanded, as if he needed to pull in a breath of fortification, then he stalked out the back door. Katy dashed forward and pressed her nose to the glass, watching until the truck disappeared into the evening shadows.

She gathered up all the dishes and ran dish water, but

she couldn't stand still long enough to get them washed. Instead, she paced the room, continually peeking out the back door and checking the clock. When would Dad return? Her chest felt tight and her hands shook. *Your will, God. Let it be Your will.* She repeated the words so many times in her head she lost count.

Finally, at 8:25, a pair of headlights turned in at the road. She stood at the back door, her hands clasped so tightly her fingers hurt. Her heart pounded so loudly she could hear it. The truck door opened, illuminating Dad briefly, but from the distance she couldn't see his face. Was he happy? Sad?

Your will, God.

Dad walked across the yard. The big light on the corner of the barn lit the path, and his shadow stretched far ahead of him, reaching the house before he did. Then he followed it onto the stoop. He gave a little jump of surprise when he stepped inside and found Katy hovering in the doorway.

She searched his face for signs of joy or despair, but he just looked like Dad. Square-jawed, clean-shaven, thick brows, serious face. She gulped out, "Well?"

Dad lowered his head and rubbed the underside of his nose with one finger. Then very slowly he lifted his chin. Katy held her breath, waiting. He met her gaze and a spark flashed in his eyes.

And even though he didn't say a word, Katy knew. She just *knew*. With a laugh of joy, Katy leaped into Dad's arms. She pressed her cheek to his chest.

He chuckled, the sound a vibration in Katy's ear. "Things'll be changing, Katy-girl."

Still nestled in his embrace, she nodded. Yes, things would change. Having a stepmother would be a new experience. But Katy knew the important things would also stay the same. *Neoteric* and same-old, same-old all at once. And somehow she didn't mind at all.

Discussion Questions for Katy's Debate

1. How do you think developing your debating skills might help you as a Christian? Should you argue with someone who has an opposing view of Christianity?

2. Katy struggled with how she felt about her father dating Mrs. Graber. Do you think Katy's father should have talked with Katy before showing his interest in Mrs. Graber? Why or why not?

3. How might Katy have handled things differently? How would you handle the emotional aspect of accepting a stepparent into your family?

4. How would you approach your parents about issues that you disagree on? What if the disagreement remains after you have had a discussion about it?

5. If you found yourself beginning to have a crush on someone you thought your parents would disapprove of, what would you do? What is more of an issue—gaining a boyfriend or gaining your parent's trust? How do you think honoring your parents comes into play?

6. Even though Katy didn't want a stepmother, she told her dad to reestablish his relationship with Mrs. Graber. Why do you think she make that choice?

7. When Katy decided having Mrs. Graber as part of their family would be both "esoteric and same-old, same-old," what did she mean? Is it possible to have new and old at the same time?

A Gift of Grace

A Novel

Amy Clipston

Rebecca Kauffman's tranquil Old Order Amish life is transformed when she suddenly has custody of her two teenage nieces after her "English" sister and brother-in-law are killed in an automobile accident. Instant motherhood, after years of unsuccessful attempts to conceive a child of her own, is both a joy and a heartache. Rebecca struggles to give the teenage girls the guidance they need as well as fulfill her duties to Daniel as an Amish wife.

Rebellious Jessica is resistant to Amish ways and constantly in trouble with the community. Younger sister Lindsay is caught in the middle, and the strain between Rebecca and Daniel mounts as Jessica's rebellion escalates. Instead of the beautiful family life she dreamed of creating for her nieces, Rebecca feels as if her world is being torn apart by two different cultures, leaving her to question her place in the Amish community, her marriage, and her faith in God.

Available in stores and online!

Katy Lambright Series

Katy's Homecoming

Kim Vogel Sawyer

Just One Perfect Night

Katy gets the chance of a lifetime—she's been elected to the homecoming court, and there are rumors her crush, Bryce, might ask her to go with him. What could be more perfect? For one unforgettable night she would be able to experience life as many other teenage girls do—a stunning gown, gorgeous hair, jewelry, and makeup. Except Katy's Mennonite community prohibits dancing as well as fancy dresses and makeup, and her father would not approve. When an opportunity arises that could allow her to attend without her father knowing, Katy must decide: Will she hold tight to her convictions, or will she sacrifice her principles for one special night?

Available in stores and online!

ZONDERVAN®
.com

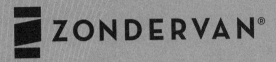

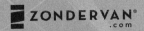